Book 2 of the Series

SOPHIE WRITES A LOVE STORY

LINDA KAY

authorHOUSE®

AuthorHouse™
1663 Liberty Drive
Bloomington, IN 47403
www.authorhouse.com
Phone: 1-800-839-8640

Published by AuthorHouse   01/07/2014

ISBN: 978-1-4969-6263-8 (sc)
ISBN: 978-1-4969-6262-1 (e)

Library of Congress Control Number: 2015900055

Any people depicted in stock imagery provided by Thinkstock are models,
and such images are being used for illustrative purposes only.
Certain stock imagery © Thinkstock.

This book is printed on acid-free paper.

Because of the dynamic nature of the Internet, any web addresses or
links contained in this book may have changed since publication and
may no longer be valid. The views expressed in this work are solely those
of the author and do not necessarily reflect the views of the publisher,
and the publisher hereby disclaims any responsibility for them.

Cover Design by Shelley Glasow Schadowsky, www.goodlifeguide.com
Edited by Janie Goltz

CONTENTS

Chapter 1   Sophie 1

Chapter 2   Sophie's Story Begins 9

Chapter 3   Sophie Writes, 1954 21

Chapter 4   Don 27

Chapter 5   Sophie and Donnie 37

Chapter 6   Don 49

Chapter 7   Sophie 59

Chapter 8   The Story Continues 64

Chapter 9   Art Lessons For Don 72

Chapter 10   Sophie and Donnie, 1954 90

Chapter 11   Sophie 101

Chapter 12   Sophie and Donnie 109

Chapter 13   Don 116

Chapter 14   Sophie 127

Chapter 15   Sophie Continues Her Story 132

Chapter 16   Sophie 137

Chapter 17   Sophie and Grace 146

Chapter 18   Holiday Times 149

Chapter 19   Sophie's Story Continues.................. 156
Chapter 20   The Story Continues 170
Chapter 21   Sophie's Story Continues................. 186
Chapter 22   Sophie's Final Chapter..................... 198
Chapter 23   The Staley Book Signing.................. 210

Acknowledgements 219
About the Author... 221

The door to the attic was heavy. As Sophie pushed up on the middle of the folding plywood pieces, she called upon all her strength to lift them. A tear stung the corner of her eye. Mumbling to herself, she scolded Carl for not being there to do this heavy task. She didn't know whether to cry because she missed him, or to cry because she was angry at him for leaving her. Sophie had always relied on her husband when they needed access to the attic.

Brushing off her hands, she stood up on the floor of the attic and pulled the chain on the light. The sun streaming in from the single window on the end of the gable was filled with a churning of dust, disturbed by her movement. The odor of musty paper filled the air.

Sophie had decided to get started on the attic clearing at the insistence of her children. She surveyed the length of the attic and smiled as she thought of her son, Tom, gently coaxing her. They both knew she needed to sort through and get rid of all unnecessary papers, as well as other "junque," as Carl had called it. Sophie dreaded the task, since so many memories of Carl were stored there, and her heart was heavy with the thought of his passing.

The first box in her path was filled with Carl's mother's papers. An easy box to mark for trash, she dragged it to the side for Tom's disposal project.

She brushed off the top of the second box and found it filled with photos. There was Trudy with her husband and kids; Tom with his family, including wife number one and wife number two; and Shirley and her brood. After glancing through some of the envelopes of pictures, she decided she would sort through these by family, put them in a sack, and give them to the kids. Since there were no plastic bags in the attic, Sophie had to make her way back down the stairs.

She was searching the kitchen closet for some grocery bags when the phone rang.

"Mom, what are you doing?" Her younger daughter Shirley's voice was cheerful.

"Oh, just getting started on the attic."

"I wondered if you are going to be home at lunch time. I thought I'd pick us up a sandwich and stop by for a visit." Working only a couple of miles from Sophie's house, Shirley had become a more frequent visitor since her father's death.

"That would be fine, honey. What time will you be here?"

"Oh, probably about 12:15. Anything special you want?"

"You can get me a chicken salad sandwich. No chips, and I have some lemonade here in the fridge."

"Perfect. I'll be by shortly after noon. Be careful climbing up and down those stairs. Did you open that heavy attic door?" she asked in a scolding tone.

"Yes, I did." Sophie picked out the plastic bags as she talked, trying not to overreact to Shirley's questions.

"Okay, well, just be careful. See you in a bit." Sophie returned the phone to the charger, and mounted the stairs to the attic.

The dividing of the pictures was a fun task, since Sophie could reminisce as she looked through each of the photos of children and grandchildren. She finished sorting, setting aside a few she wanted to keep for herself.

An old trunk stood alone at one end of the attic. It probably hadn't been opened for years. She wiped off the dust and released the latches to raise the lid. The odor of old clothing, mothballs, and papers permeated the air as she leaned over its contents. On top was a favorite dress she had worn to Shirley's wedding, one that Carl really liked. Its green satin was faded to a dingy tan, so it was obviously ready for the trash pile. Boxes contained memories from each of her children: school report cards and newspaper articles of interest. These could go in with the pictures.

Her wedding gown was sealed in a plastic bag, but the years had taken their toll. The gown was yellowed, and the lace was almost a coffee color. She removed the fragile garment from the bag and held it in front of her, twirling around in a slow waltz, closing her eyes and thinking of Carl. An old white, leather-bound album of wedding pictures was complete with a small music box at the top that played the wedding march. Carl was so handsome in his suit. The black-and-white pictures didn't do justice to those brown eyes that had captivated Sophie all those years ago. A lump caught in her throat. She flipped the pages and wondered about all the friends who had been a part of the wedding. Where were they all now?

Sophie found her album of high school friends, and articles of interest, thumbed through them, and smiled as she thought of how much fun these would be for the next class reunion.

Then a small wooden box tucked into one corner of the chest caught her eye. Sophie carefully laid aside the other articles, picked up the box, and cradled it in her hand. Slowly, she lifted the lid on the box to see the small ring woven of twine, along with a tarnished silver chain.

"Mom, are you upstairs?" Shirley had arrived.

Sophie jumped at Shirley's voice. "Coming, dear." She quickly took both items out of the box and placed them in her pocket, as though she were a child caught with her hand in the cookie jar. She walked carefully down the stairs, her mind lost in an old memory.

"How's the attic cleaning coming along?"

"I'm afraid it's going to take me a long time. But I guess that's one thing I have plenty of, right?"

"Sounds like fun." Shirley sat down at the table.

Sophie brought the lemonade and poured it over ice.

"You look great, Mom," Shirley said, nibbling at her sandwich.

"Why, thanks, honey." Sophie smiled. "I feel good." She paused a moment, her mind barely in the present. "You know, it's been a long time, but I think I might start writing again."

"That's great. I worry about you some, with Dad gone. I don't want you to be lonely."

"I keep your dad's picture out on the lamp table in the living room. When I'm lonely, I talk to him about things. I'm sure he's listening. You know I have some good friends and neighbors as well." Sophie did not want Shirley hovering over her. "I'm really not anxious to get rid of the house, you know, but I understand why you kids want me to be in a smaller place."

"It would be great if you could downsize and clean out the stuff here in the house that's been laying around for years and years. Have you found any real treasures?" Shirley finished her sandwich.

"Nothing special so far." Sophie reached into her pocket and turned the two small items between her fingers, feeling their texture. "There's an old trunk up there and some other boxes of stuff, as well as Christmas decorations and old clothes. But I'll get through it. I'm going to go up there every morning until I get it done."

"Will you call me if you need anything?" Shirley reached over and put her hand on her mother's arm.

Sophie patted her hand. "I will, honey. You just don't worry about me. I can still take care of myself."

"Mom, have you looked at those brochures I brought over last time about the retirement villas? It looks like a really nice place with lots of activities."

Sophie quickly changed the subject, as she felt her face flush at Shirley's comments. "Thanks for bringing lunch, Shirley. You probably need to get back to work." She was anxious for her daughter to be on her way.

Shirley stood up and pushed her chair back.

"Heard anything from Trudy?" Shirley stopped at the door.

"She calls me quite a bit. All of you have been really good at keeping in touch since your dad died."

"I'll give my big sis a call this week. See you later, Mom." Shirley hugged Sophie and kissed her on the cheek. "Take care. Love you!"

Sophie watched as Shirley pulled out of the driveway, making sure she was gone. A squirrel ran down the tree and across the yard, carrying an acorn from the tall oak. Several of them scampered about outside on the lawn, getting ready for winter. Sophie watched momentarily as the small, furry animal buried his prize, digging into the soft soil.

She took her two treasures from her pocket and laid them on the dining room table, pondering where she may have put the old journals she had kept. On the top shelf of the guest bedroom closet, she found the box, covered with dust, and removed the lid to find several small journals. She had never shared these with anyone. Her pulse quickened as she thought about what she might have written so many years ago. Each of the journals was dated on the outside cover, so Sophie arranged them by the dates written. The first journal contained entries that were written by her mother, followed later by entries that looked to be from when Sophie was just beginning to use cursive, as the letters were large and bold. As a young girl of ten, based on the dates of the journal, she had for some time recorded her story.

"I ought to write a book from these journals!" she said aloud, feeling a rush of adrenaline at the prospect. "It would be fun to create 'my story'".

And somewhere, buried in the journals, was an account of the woven ring and chain.

Chapter 2

SOPHIE'S STORY BEGINS

My mother wrote the first of the journals to tell the story of my youth. Here are a few excerpts:

July 17, 1943. This is the beginning of a journal that I hope my daughter will continue when she is old enough to write. Hitler is leading Germany, and many of the words now emblazoned in history are formed: Gestapo, Dachau concentration camp. Germany had captured Rome, Mussolini was deposed, the Allies defeated the Germans in North Africa, and the War rages on. It was during all these historic events that Sophie Palmer was born, the second child and first daughter to James and Ellen Palmer, in a small Midwestern hospital. She is the most beautiful baby I've ever seen. Because of the rationing, Sophie earned us an extra supply of sugar and staples. We took Sophie home to the farm where she met her brother, Daniel. The farm consists of prime acreage and a small timber along the northeast side of the property. Jim raises cattle and pigs, along with the usual corn and soybeans.

July 17, 1947 - Today is Sophie's fourth birthday. The war is over, and things are getting back to normal here on the farm. We celebrated with cake and ice cream and had the Grandmas and Grandpas here to help us celebrate. Dan helped her blow out the candles. Grandma Palmer gave Sophie a book and read her a story from it in the afternoon. She is very interested in books. She asked her Grandpa Palmer to tell her a story, so he had Sophie give him three people or things to get him started. The story was a wonderful adventure that included Sophie, Dan, and the Big Bad Wolf. It seems this has become a special game for Sophie.

July 17, 1949 - Sophie will be starting school in August. She is so excited at the prospect, because her brother gets to go every day. We've started giving her an allowance for some chores on the farm, and she helps me in the house as well. Her favorite is working in the flower beds and enjoying the flowers. She doesn't like to get dirt under her fingernails, but loves watering and spraying with bug killers.

July 17, 1951 - Sophie has some friends from school to help her celebrate her birthday. She has a wonderful, caring personality and is getting good grades in school, especially in spelling and writing. Her teacher is amazed at her ability to put together a story. I've shared with her teacher the game she plays with her Grandpa Palmer, which has no doubt contributed to her creativity. She is now learning to write in cursive, and it is coming along, but with very large letters.

July 17, 1953 - Sophie is now ten years old. Her birthday was celebrated with a slumber party with her friends. Now in fifth grade, Sophie is blossoming into a lovely girl and wears her strawberry blonde hair long. It's sometimes in a ponytail. She knows that I have been writing down some things each birthday, and is curious about writing and keeping the journal going forward. So I think it's time to turn the journal over to Sophie.

Mother was a great homemaker and raised a beautiful garden each year. As Dan and I played, we would sometimes raid the garden for carrots and onions to use in making mud pies or fixing dinner plates for the cats and dogs. We were never short on imagination.

However, this imagination would sometimes get us into trouble.

Each of us had a responsibility for chores. I was in charge of the chickens, both the baby chicks in the spring and the older chickens as they started laying eggs. I have fond memories of those fuzzy little yellow chicks in a box from the local hatchery. I fed and watered them, mourned those that died, and buried them carefully in the chicken yard. As they developed white wing feathers, the chicks were released out into the world. In just a few more weeks and with a full coat of feathers, some would eventually become targets for Sunday dinner.

Dan's chores were with the pigs and cattle, giving them hay and feed from the feed bin in the barn, and making sure the water tanks were full.

Spring and summer were great times, as Dan and I had ample time to explore the territory surrounding the farm. We would squat down in the ditches along the country roads and harvest wild strawberries, carrying buckets made of coffee cans with wire handles on our bicycles. Mother made jam with these berries, more flavorful than any purchased at the store. There was a creek running through the timber, with many places for secret hideouts. There was a small spillway over the concrete under the gravel road, and we dubbed it "Little Niagara."

Winters were very cold with mountains of snow that piled far over the hedge rows. The crusts on these drifts were hard enough to walk on, but also made great walls and roofs for tunneled-out houses in the snow. Childhood offered me an endless adventure, one from which I would find myself creating a memory to last a lifetime.

Sophie stopped typing and backed away from the computer. Her mother had been so helpful to write the introduction of the journals to set up the recording of her life. The first pages told a story of Sophie's early years on the farm. They were poignant in their description, and all her pets had been identified by name. These entries were fairly brief. Following her mother's notes, Sophie had begun to write more descriptive entries.

Sophie read on into the first journal, and found descriptions of events she could actually remember happening. She had described the county fair in the summer, with her chickens in the wire cages and Dan's pigs in the pens, and the cacophony of animal noises around them. Dan had to lead a pig around the arena using a cane, which was no easy task. She had described the township center where their 4-H club met for their monthly demonstrations and reports. Sophie could still hear the footsteps echoing on the wooden floors of the building. A long table was placed at the front of the room for officers of the club. Demonstrations from its members on anything from gardening to sewing to flower arranging, were done at the front of the room, as well as small animal care.

In addition to the description of the 4-H hall and the county fair, Sophie had added some highlights of the work she and Dan had done to create a "hideout" in the timber. Dan had cut branches from the trees, and they had together created a make-shift house. Pine needles and leaves served to create the floor of the house. Twine string from the hay bales was used as a hinge to hold up a door made of branches that swung shut over the doorway into the hut. From inside the house, the two of them had confiscated any unused utensil or pot and pan they could find around the house and barn to use. Dan had created benches to sit on by dragging out some straw bales from the barn. The descriptions of these items in the journal were so vivid, that Sophie could picture all of it in her mind, and she smiled at their ingenuity. She and Dan were really a team, but he was definitely the creative builder.

 14

Sophie stood up, and started toward the kitchen when the phone rang. This time it was Tom calling.

"Mom? What's up?" he asked.

"Nothing much. What about you?"

"I just wanted to call to see if you are making some progress in getting things ready for me to take to Goodwill or the dump this weekend."

"I'm working on it, Tom. I was up in the attic today, and I've got some piles sorted out for you. Some things I want to give to you and the girls, and some are ready to be thrown away." Sophie carried her phone with her as she talked.

"Okay. Is everything all right?"

"I'm fine. Don't worry about me. You just look after that family of yours." Sophie didn't mean to sound like she was scolding him, but she had already dealt with Shirley's hovering today.

"I'll be over on Saturday to take out anything that's ready to go. See you then!"

Sophie mused that her children thought she couldn't do anything without them. What did they think she had been doing all these years while they had been too busy to stop by? She felt irritated with her children.

She returned to the journal, reading further into the small book, filled with short notes about life on the farm. It was when she got to the second journal and

Linda Kay

the year 1954 that she found the notes she had been looking for. The year started out with a description of winter weather in January, school events in February and March, notes on friends and Easter vacation in April, and the arrival of spring in May. School was dismissed for the summer in late May, and the journal made reference to the school bus ride home on the last day of school. Tommy Jackson had been tormenting her by pulling her hair on the bus.

At the age of 10, apparently I had taken over the writing in the journal.

June 10, 1954 – Today I went to the hideout in the timber to read a book and just be alone. As I was sitting inside the hut, someone called out. It scared me at first, until I realized it was a boy about my age. He introduced himself as Donnie, and he is visiting his aunt and uncle who live on the other side of the creek from our farm. He doesn't usually come to the farm, but his parents are on a long trip. I invited him into the hut and we talked for a little while. He said his aunt would be looking for him, so he didn't stay long, but we agreed to meet again tomorrow.

June 11, 1954 – Donnie came back to the hideout today, and brought along his little dog, Sammy. He's going to be at his aunt's house for a couple of weeks. We walked around some in the timber, and he showed me the poison ivy. He also knows a lot about trees, and he could name almost every one of them. Donnie is 12 years old. He has dark curly hair, brown eyes, and he talks a little funny. He lives with his parents in Chicago, and he never gets to be in the timber there; just concrete and big buildings he says, except for the parks. Donnie brought along a canvas from his aunt's house to throw over the roof of the hut.

June 12, 1954 – We met at the hideout again today, and we walked back to my house, so he could meet my mom and dad. Dad says he looks a lot like his father, who is our neighbor's brother. Dad knew him when he was in school. Donnie took Dan's bike and I rode mine, and we went down by the creek that runs through the timber between the two farms. We caught some tadpoles and found some really neat rocks buried under the moss in the creek. It started raining in the afternoon, so we rode our bikes back really fast so Donnie could get back to his aunt's house.

June 13, 1954 – It's still raining – "cats and dogs," as Grandma says. Donnie called me, and we talked for just a little while. We decided that we would go to the hideout tomorrow, even if it's still raining. I'm going to take along a flashlight and make us a sack lunch. I'll fix a thermos of iced tea, put together some sandwiches, and bag up some cookies. Since the hut has the canvas over the top, it might be pretty dry in there.

Sophie looked at her watch and noted the time – already 9:00 PM and she had a favorite program she wanted to watch. She put the journal aside, marking the page with her emery board, and switched on the television, rubbing her eyes. The show was a rerun, so she switched off the television and let her mind wander back in time to those three days in her journal. She could still remember when Donnie first entered her hideout. She had liked him immediately. That evening she had told her parents about their meeting. She remembered the little dog, Sam. He was a Schnauzer, really a cute dog. In the country, dogs weren't cut and trimmed like Sam. They were lucky to get a bath now and then.

The day they rode the bicycles, Sophie had gotten a bad sunburn on her neck and upper arms. She had always burned pretty easily, and they were out in the sun for a long time before it got cloudy and started to rain.

Sophie picked up the small woven ring and held it between her fingers, studying the weave. What had happened to Donnie? Jack and Edna had told her folks that Donnie had gone to high school in Chicago, and then had gone to college somewhere out in Iowa. But by then, Sophie had other things happening in her own life, and memories of Donnie had faded with new friends and events.

She spent a few moments preparing for bed, noticing the soft lines in her face and the touch of gray in her hair. She decided she needed to see Cori about the highlights in her hair. She held in her stomach and turned sideways, then back to face the mirror. She could stand to lose five pounds. Finally retiring to her bedroom, she had trouble falling asleep, her mind consumed with putting her memories on paper and creating a story for others to enjoy, a story of her summer adventure with Donnie, her first boyfriend. Despite her frustration at her insomnia, she felt more

Linda Kay

energized and alive than she had felt in some time. She flipped on the light in the small office, and switched on the computer. The only way to put her mind to rest was to start typing.

Chapter 3
SOPHIE WRITES, 1954

The rain continued to come down in torrents, with a wind blowing the raindrops such that they appeared to be coming down sideways. I made some sandwiches, put some iced tea into a Thermos, selected some cookies for a small container, and packed everything into a lunch box. I was getting stir-crazy sitting in the house all day, and Dan was really getting on my nerves. I placed a quick call to Donnie, and we agreed to meet at the hideout. I found my rubber boots and a raincoat, as well as my umbrella, and started out for the woods. "Mom, I'll be back. I'm meeting Donnie at the timber."

"It's pouring down rain, Sophie. What on earth do you want to go out in this for?"

"We have a tarp over the hideout, and I have some things for lunch. I won't be gone long."

"You be careful. There might be places where the mud is really soft out there. And be sure to get back here before dark!"

"I will. Bye!" I was out the door and splashing across the gravel drive, making my way to the pasture, and feeling more like a duck than a girl.

The rain and the wind were stronger than I had expected, and my umbrella turned inside out in the wind. I quickly pulled it back into place, and held on to one corner of it, looping the handle of the lunch box over my arm. The pasture was muddy and had standing water in several places. I made my way around these puddles, sloshing through some of the shallower ones on my way. Within a few minutes, I arrived at the clearing in front of the hideout, where I saw Donnie just ducking inside.

"Think it will rain?" I asked as I entered the small shelter right behind him.

"I can't believe how much it rained. The creek is really full. I had to come across the bridge, 'cause the water is too deep and running kind of fast." Donnie gestured toward the direction of the bridge. "It took me longer to get here that way."

"I came across the pasture around some of the lakes that are out there!" It was important to make my journey just as exciting as Donnie's. I set the lunch box down on the floor of the hideout, still somewhat dry under its makeshift roof. Luckily the shelter had been built on higher ground.

"What's in your lunch box?" asked Donnie, sitting down cross-legged on the ground.

"Just some sandwiches and cookies and some iced tea. I'll set them out on the table." I smiled at him as I started to unpack the lunch onto the plywood Dan had placed on top of a bale of straw to serve as a table for us. Then I sat down across from Donnie.

"Help yourself."

"What have you been up to?" Donnie asked as he unwrapped a ham and cheese on wheat.

"Just doing stuff around the house. I started a jigsaw puzzle yesterday. Dan helped me with it for a while, but we got into it. He is such a pain in the neck sometimes. Anyway, it's a picture of a Model T car and lots of people and buildings. There are so many pieces that it will take us a while to get it together. Want to help me with it?" I would certainly welcome Donnie's help.

"Puzzles aren't my thing. I've been helping my uncle with some stuff around the farm, working out in the barn some and in the fields. He even paid me for helping him! It's really hard work, though, and I just pass out quickly at night. Do you read a lot?"

"Oh, yes. I love to read. And I like to write, too. I write some poems and sometimes some stories. It's fun." I poured us both some iced tea into the cups I had brought along.

"What do you write about?" Donnie asked.

"I write about happy things mostly, some about my dog or other animals on the farm."

"I like westerns and mysteries, so I read sometimes. I like to draw. My mom's a painter, and she does some really neat stuff. She says I have some 'natural talent', and she'll teach me more." Donnie finished his sandwich and took a cookie from the cookie bag. "This really tastes good, Sophie. Thanks!"

"You're welcome. What's that noise?" I frowned and listened to the sound of the rain on the tarp. It seemed to grow louder.

"I think it's just the rain, and the wind through the trees, probably. Let's take a look outside." Donnie motioned for me to follow him out the entrance.

We stepped outside and looked up into the trees. The noise was growing louder, and sounded like a roar, like a train was passing through the area. But there wasn't a train track for miles. We looked across the creek toward Jack and Edna's house in time to see the tail of a tornado reaching down from the clouds, heading directly toward the farm.

"Look at that!" cried Donnie. We stood for a moment, frozen in fear. "I've never seen anything like that before!"

"Me either! What should we do?" I was so afraid, I grasped Donnie's arm.

"I think we need to stay right here in the trees. Let's get inside the hideout and squat down by that bale of straw that's in there!"

We ran back into the shelter and huddled next to the straw. The sound of the oncoming tornado grew louder as it roared past the farm and across the timber. The rain continued to pound the tarp on the shelter, and both of us were really scared. The sides of the tarp rose and fell with the pressure from the storm. When the roaring stopped, we looked at each other, not saying a word for a few moments.

"Do you think it's gone?" I asked, my voice trembling.

"I don't know. Are you afraid to look outside to see what's been going on?" Donnie stood and walked to the opening.

We stepped outside gingerly and looked toward his uncle's farm. There was debris scattered across the field, and the roof to the machine shed was gone. A small hog shed had been moved out into the middle of the field, and a chicken house was almost completely flat.

"I need to get back there to see if everyone is okay," said Donnie, starting to walk in the direction of the bridge over the creek.

"I'll go with you." I was hurrying to catch up with him. His legs were much longer than mine, and it was hard to keep up. "I'm right behind you."

We hurried down the pathway to the bridge. As we drew near the bridge, with only a few yards left to go, we looked up to see a huge wall of water surging toward us.

Chapter 4
DON

He removed his raincoat and his hat and hung them on the coat tree in one corner of the restaurant. Umbrella still in hand, he walked to a small table along the far wall, close to the end of the counter. The aroma of bacon and eggs filled the air.

"Morning, Don," the waitress called out to him as she walked by the coffee urn to fill up a pot.

"Mornin'," he replied, taking his seat, and placing his folded umbrella under the table by the wall. "I'm putting this here, so don't let me forget it."

"Gotcha!" She poured a cup of coffee into the mug she had retrieved from the shelf behind the counter. "Know what you want this morning?"

"I'm not sure; just bring me a menu, will you?" He took the cup in his right hand and took a quick sip of the coffee while waiting for the menu. "Suzy, you can bring me a glass of juice on your way back," he said over his shoulder.

Suzy returned with the menu and the glass of juice. "I'll be back in a few," she said as she took out her order book and walked to the next table.

"Why is even ordering breakfast such a hard job?" he mumbled to himself. Don Ribold had come to realize that he was probably depressed, and he was at his wits end to know what to do about it, short of making a trip to the doctor. Living alone, he found all tasks to be overwhelming, whether it was keeping the place clean, doing laundry, or shopping. Cooking offered him no pleasure, preparing meals for only one. He sighed, laid down the menu, and picked up his coffee mug.

He looked around the restaurant for any familiar faces, but saw none. The restaurant was full of folks on their way to work, just stopping for a quick breakfast and a cup of coffee. Checkered table cloths covered the tables. Various antiques and collectibles were hung haphazardly along the walls. The older patrons would remember these items from their own childhood. Posters bore ads for products long since discontinued, and metal signs boasted business names from another era in the life of the city. It occurred to him that he and the hangings were all by-goners.

Suzy returned to his table. "Know what you want now?"

"I'll have two eggs, over medium, with rye toast and hash browns. And bacon." He handed her the menu, realizing his order was the same as any other morning, and managed a slight smile. She was a good waitress. A man walked across the room toward Don.

He stood up to greet him, "Jerry Cole! How are you?"

"Please, sit down. May I join you?"

"Sure, I've already ordered breakfast, but I'm sure Suzy will be back around shortly. What have you been up to?" Don was truly glad to see Jerry. Jerry had worked with him at the insurance office. He was an aggressive salesman, bringing in a large portfolio of policies.

"Same old, same old. Business is good, and I'm right on target for my goals for this year. So, no complaints. Question is, how are you doing?"

"I'm getting by." Don wasn't eager to share his true feelings with Jerry.

"What do you mean, you're getting by? You are Don Ribold. Don Ribold doesn't just 'get by.'" Jerry shook his head.

"I'm like a ship without a rudder at the moment, Jerry. Since Arlene died, I've had trouble getting on with my life. My son Marty is busy, and he and his family don't really have time to spend with me. The grandkids are busy with school. I go to most of the ballgames and track meets." Despite his reserve, Don poured out his feelings.

Suzy came back to take Jerry's order for breakfast. "Just one pancake, some sausage, and lots of coffee for me, thanks," he instructed her.

Jerry looked at his friend. "Don, this just doesn't sound like you. You surely have some interests you have saved for your retirement," he said, emptying a creamer into his coffee mug. "You were my mentor and my idol when we were working together."

"I used to look forward to retirement. Golf and reading were my main interests, both of which I have done this summer. I have a couple of collections of coins and old farm tools. But it's just not enough to pique my interest. Maybe I shouldn't have quit working when I did, but Arlene needed me at home." He looked down at the food.

"Do you have any hobbies, like photography or painting?" Don watched Jerry drop a dollop of butter on his pancake.

"Years ago I did some painting, but haven't picked up a brush in probably thirty years. I wouldn't know where to start. As for photography, I'm not anxious to put out the money for the kind of equipment I'd like to have. My camera is an old 35mm." He looked toward the window, as though some inspiration might come to him from the street or sidewalk outside.

"Painting? I have just the person you need to meet. My new insurance client is opening an art supply store out at the mall. He has everything imaginable in the store for painting, and he gives classes three nights a week. I think I have his business card in my wallet." Jerry put down his fork and reached into his hip pocket for his wallet, sorting through business cards and pulling out just one. He handed the card to Don.

"Impressions by Charles. Charles Orman, President. Okay, so tell me about this Charles Orman."

"Chuck is an incredible artist, and has been teaching at the college for some time. He decided to get out on his own, where he can teach and sell his work. I think he'll do a great job with the business, since he has so many facets from which to draw revenues. You should talk to him and get into his class. Who knows, you might be the next Monet!" Jerry smiled at his friend.

"Right!" Don smirked in response. "But I will stop by to see him. Is his store open yet?"

"It's not open as yet, but if you stop by there, I'm sure he'll be in there working on it, getting ready for opening day. Just tell him I sent you."

They finished their breakfast and chatted about events at the insurance office and various clients they had worked with in the past.

"Don, it's been good to visit with you. Go see Chuck, as it might give you something to look forward to, okay?"

"Yeah, good to see you, too. And thanks, Jerry." Don extended his hand. They had been good friends.

Jerry left for work, and Don enjoyed another cup of coffee from Suzy's bottomless pot. Many of the patrons had left the restaurant for work, leaving only those with no agenda. Don looked at the card Jerry had given him. Well, he'd think about it. He left a tip for Suzy on the table and tucked the business card into his wallet.

Don had made a practice of walking to the diner for breakfast, although it was a good mile and a half away from his condo. The walk back took him past many businesses just opening for the day. A bookstore was a favorite of his, as he loved to see the new books on the shelves and the ads for the current best sellers. Sometimes he would pick up a magazine to read or a crossword puzzle book to occupy his time.

Ben greeted Don as he opened the door to the shop. "Hi there, stranger. Haven't seen you in a while."

"I've just been hangin' around. Ben, what do you have in books on painting or watercolor?" Don was curious to see what was available.

"Over in the Arts section there are some instruction books. And there are always those picture books with lots of art projects in them." Ben motioned in the two directions for Don.

Don wandered back into the Arts section and looked at what was available. One of particular interest seemed to clearly describe the necessary supplies and techniques for paintings, so Don tucked it under his arm and continued looking through the shelves. Then he walked to the 'coffee table books' section to see what other artists had produced for print in the books. As he thumbed through the pages, he thought he might be too old to start something like this. He decided to buy the book he had found, and took it to the counter where Ben was looking over some tickets from the previous day.

"Find what you were looking for, Don?" he asked, as Don laid the book on the counter.

"I think so. I used to do some painting, so I thought I'd read up on this. Just something to do." He took out the card Jerry had given him. "Do you know this guy?" he asked Ben.

"Chuck Orman? Sure, I know Chuck. I heard he is opening his own business, but this is the first time I've seen his card. He's a good guy. Do you know him?"

"Not yet, I don't. But I may stop by to see him, just to find out what he has in the store and talk to him a little. How much do I owe you?"

"That'll be fifteen dollars and ninety-nine cents with tax. Hope you enjoy the book." Ben placed the book in a bag.

"Just keep the penny. I feel generous today." Don smiled at Ben, and picked up his package. He stopped by the display of new books to see if there was anything of interest, then finally headed out the door.

"Have a good day!" Ben called out to Don as he left the store.

"Everybody always says that. Have a good day. It's just another day," he muttered to himself.

He trudged down the street toward his apartment. The trees were turning colors, and he could feel autumn in the air as he walked. He zipped up his jacket, tucked the book under his arm, and plunged his hands into his pockets.

Don pressed the security buttons with his password, and unlocked the door to the building. He checked his mailbox and picked up his newspaper, mounted the stairs to the second floor. As he opened the door, he noticed a chill in the air. He had left a window open last night, and it felt cold to him. The heat had not been turned on as yet, so he set the dial on the thermostat, walking to the window to crank it shut and latch it. Within a few moments, the air felt warmer.

The condo had a large living room with a fireplace and two windows that looked out into a courtyard below. Arlene had personally chosen the furniture and drapes for the room. Don had always been happy with whatever Arlene picked out, having no sense of décor himself. The kitchen was fairly small, with a breakfast bar that opened into the living room.

Don threw his keys onto the breakfast bar, along with his package from the bookstore. He noted that he hadn't yet made his bed this morning, so he threw the covers up over the pillows and left it that way. No one would be there to care about an unmade bed.

Out in the kitchen, he put on a small pot of coffee, and looked into the refrigerator to see what he might have for lunch and dinner. Nothing looked good to him. Maybe he would just order Chinese for dinner, and eat some cheese or something for lunch. He picked up the book on the counter, and took it to his recliner in the living room.

The morning sun was streaming in through the windows, making the room bright and cheerful, but Don turned on the lamp beside the recliner, and walked to the windows to pull the drapes. "Too bright," he thought to himself as the drapes closed on the traverse rod.

As he settled into the recliner, he opened the book to the first pages, scanned them, and wondered if he could still paint. He looked away for a moment, remembering his classes in art at college, and the paintings he had done for the displays in the student union and the exhibit hall. Somewhere in the house there were a few of his paintings still framed, but Arlene hadn't liked them for her decorating style. They must be up in the attic or in the building storage unit. He'd have to look for them.

Don looked through the book. He decided he would have to do something to get out of his rut. Tomorrow he would go to see Chuck Orman. If nothing else, it would be good to meet someone new.

Chapter 5
SOPHIE AND DONNIE

Sophie's Story

"Run, Sophie!" Donnie grabbed my hand, and started to run up the hill away from the creek. "Don't let go of my hand!" But we were too late. The wall of water slammed into our small bodies and tossed them like dolls in its wake. I felt Donnie's hand slipping from my grasp. I felt objects scrap my skin, thump against my knees and legs, and the force of the water in my nose and ears. Fighting against the panic that was gripping me, I held my breath and tried to tread water, hoping to break the surface. The water was dark and murky, and I couldn't see anything but blackness. I had no idea which way was up, as the water tumbled me, dragged me along the bottom, then pushed me up toward the surface. I knew I would have to try to gulp some air in one of those cycles.

Suddenly, I was on the surface of the water, moving with the force along the top at break-neck speed. I gasped for air and tried to swim, but my efforts were useless against the power of the rapids. I caught a glimpse ahead of a large tree hanging out over the water, and realized that if I could just reach that branch, I might be able to pull myself out of the torrent. Swimming to stay afloat, and angling to the right of the flooding waters, I prayed silently that the surge would push me high enough to grab the branch.

Swells moved me up and down, sometimes sucking me under the water. My arms ached from the swimming and struggling. I knew I had already swallowed a lot of the dirty water, and was also aware that I would not be able to hold myself at the surface much longer. The flood pushed me once more up with its swell, just in time for me to reach out and grab the branch of the tree. The force jerked my arms, as I struggled to hold on. Pulling with all my might, I maneuvered myself up to my chest on the branch, and hoisted one leg up, then the other, onto the branch for support. Like a sloth, I hung there with the swirling and churning waters rushing by beneath me. The roar of the water was deafening. Where was Donnie?

"Donnie!" I called out. I wasn't sure if I could hear him if he answered me, above the sound of the water.

"Donnie!" I called again. No answer.

I looked down at the water, then up at the branch, trying to decide what to do next. I couldn't just hang there indefinitely. My hands burned from holding on. The tree branch drooped suddenly, placing me within inches of the water. I decided to make my way to the base of the branch, then down the trunk of the tree, until I could reach ground. Then maybe it would be possible to wade out of the water to safety.

Slowly, moving my feet first, then my hands, I moved to the heavier part of the branch. My hands were bleeding and the bark of the tree was rough against the raw cuts. A huge bruise was forming on my right shin, along with numerous cuts and scrapes. Ignoring the pain I continued a slow, careful movement, the water still flowing endlessly beneath me.

"Sophie!" I heard my name being called in the distance. I had no idea how far I had traveled down the creek or where I was, completely disoriented. I stopped moving and listened.

"Sophie, where are you?" It was Donnie, for sure. I strained to get my bearings to determine the direction of his voice, all my senses on alert.

"Donnie, is that you?" I shouted, and listened for Donnie to call back again. This time the voice seemed a bit louder. Maybe the water was slowing its rush.

"Sophie, I-I can't see you. Where are you? I think my leg is broken!" Donnie called out, obviously suffering a great deal of pain.

"I can hear you, but I can't see you. Stay where you are, and I'll see if I can get to you. I'm stuck in a tree!" I thought momentarily that it must have sounded ridiculous to Donnie, from wherever he was. "I'll call out for you in a few minutes."

I continued moving toward the base of the branch, now with more adrenaline pumping than before. I reached the thicker part of the branch, but needed to push myself up onto the top of the branch to get a better perspective. Gathering up all my strength, I threw my arm over the branch until I could grasp the limb to pull myself up on top of it. The cuts and scrapes on my legs screamed in protest, as they were further ruptured from the climbing. Finally, on top the branch and near the trunk of the tree, I could see how far I was from the water below, and where the grass at the edge of the water started. The water still moved very rapidly, and there were logs and many other objects racing along on top the water, slamming into rocks and trees along the path. The shore line was at least ten feet away from the tree, and I had no idea of the depth of the swirling water.

Another branch of the tree reached out in the other direction, toward the shore. If I could swing to the shallower water, away from the path of the flooding, I might be safer. I slowly inched myself around the trunk of the tree and out onto the opposite branch. Lowering myself into the former sloth position, dangling from beneath the branch, I began moving out toward the narrower end. The branch sagged with the weight, lowering me nearer the water as I reached out farther. Finally, I decided I would have to take my chances and drop into the water, ready to swim for the shore if I couldn't stand up.

Holding my breath, I let go of the branch, trying to swing out toward the shore. I dropped into the water, my feet landing on sharp rocks and branches. I cried out in pain from the sudden impact, but was able to stand up and wade heavily through the shallower water, each step painful on now bare feet. Finally out of the water, I lay down on the ground and cried, the pouring rain continuing to pelt my body.

Looking back at the water, I could see that the width of the surge of water in the creek had become narrower, but the force of the water was still treacherous. Then I remembered Donnie and his desperate call for help.

"Donnie! Where are you?" I called out to him, hoping he could hear me above the roar of the water.

"Sophie! I-I can't move. Where are you?" Donnie called back, his voice trembling as though he was about to cry.

"Give me a couple of minutes, and I'll try to follow your voice to get closer to you!" I started to move in the direction of Donnie's voice. The pain in my feet was excruciating.   The bruise on my leg was getting blacker, and my arms were raw with cuts.

On the top of a small knoll along the edge of the water, there was a better view of the sides of the rushing water of the creek. I saw Donnie about 30 yards on the other side of the knoll, pinned under a tree trunk at the edge of the water. The tree had been uprooted by the force of the flood, and lay half in and half out of the water. I worked my way down the opposite side of the knoll to get closer to Donnie.

"I see you, and I'm coming!"

"Hurry!" he shouted. "I can't move the tree trunk off my leg!" He struggled with his free foot to push the trunk of the tree off his pinned leg, to no avail.

I was assessing the situation as I approached Donnie. The roots of the tree were sticking out of the water at the base of the trunk. The trunk had fallen away from the water in the surge, and its trunk lay partially in the water with its branches on the grass of the bank. Donnie was wedged under the trunk of the tree, his right leg buried in the mud.

"Oh, no! You are really trapped under that tree trunk! How are we going to move it?" I squatted down beside him. "Are you okay?"

"Well, no! I can't get the tree trunk to move at all with my other foot. Sophie, can you help me try to move it?" Donnie was frantic to free his leg.

I placed my shoulder against the trunk of the tree, and Donnie braced his left foot above his right leg. Together we pushed with all our strength, but the tree trunk would not move.

"I have a better idea," I said. "If I can find something to dig with, I can dig down beneath your leg, and maybe we can free you that way." Surely something might work as a shovel or spade to dig out the mud beneath Donnie's leg. I spotted a piece of log on the bank that was hollowed out and broken, and started to dig down into the mud. The water continued to recede into the banks of the creek, leaving behind a trail of debris. My hands hurt with each shove made with the wood into the mud. Once Donnie cried out when I got close to his leg with the digging. I moved to the opposite side of the tree trunk to dig out near his foot, so we could pull him out from under the tree.

"Sophie, I'm so sorry I can't help you," Donnie said, choking back tears and trying to be calm.

"I think I've just about got enough dug out to try to pull you out from under the tree." I walked around to where Donnie lay, and surveyed the position of the leg. "If I pull you straight out, and you help push with your other leg, we might be able to wriggle you out of there."

I grabbed Donnie under the arms and began to pull; digging my heels into the mud. I slipped and slid in the mud, and struggled to gain leverage to pull. Donnie was pushing with his left foot, but was racked with pain from the suction of the mud on his leg.

"Sophie, I have to rest a minute. It really hurts!" Donnie lay back and took some deep breaths, trying to gather his courage to continue.

"Okay, let's try one more time," he said. I pulled and he pushed, and we finally were able to get enough leverage to pull him out from beneath the tree trunk, his right leg totally useless.

Exhausted, I plopped back against the embankment, breathing deeply but exhilarated from the accomplishment. "We made it!" I exclaimed, my face and hands covered with mud.

"Thank you, Sophie. You are a life-saver! What do we do now?" Donnie realized that even though we had freed him, we were still in danger, and he wasn't able to walk.

"I'll check things out to see where we are and what's around here. Do you have any idea how far the water carried us?" I stood up on sore feet and started walking toward the top of the bank, reaching out to level myself while climbing.

"I don't know this area well enough to have any idea. It seemed like we were in the water for a long time, but I don't know that for sure." Donnie was more than a little dazed by the experience and the pain he was feeling.

"I can't see your aunt and uncle's farm at all. It's going to get dark before too long, so we need to get to a safe place." I walked stealthily down the bank and back to Donnie. "If you can dig in your left foot to push, I can pull you, and we might be able to get you to the top of the hill and away from the water. Can you help me?"

"I'll do my best." Donnie rose up on his elbows and dug his heel into the ground.

Positioning myself behind him, I grabbed him under his arms, pulling with all my strength to move him up the hill. Somehow we managed to move Donnie to the top.

"I'm going to look around to see if I can find anything to put around your leg to brace it. Then we need to see if we can find some sort of shelter, as it's going to get dark pretty quickly. I wish it would stop raining!" I placed my hands on my hips and started to walk away.

"Sophie, don't go too far away. You need to be able to find your way back here."

"Don't worry. I'll not be far away. I'll see what I can find."

Down the hill I began to look for sticks and twine or whatever might be useful in binding up the broken leg. Just a few yards away, there were remains of a small building, apparently a hog house blown away from a farm in the tornado. It was upright, but sitting in a ditch with water running under it. If I walked the small building, turning it as I moved it up the hill and away from the water, I could manage it. Picking up some sturdy branches and some cloth, I returned to Donnie with my find.

"Look what I found! Any chance you might have a pocket knife?"

"I do have one." He reached into his pocket and pulled out a knife with various blade sizes and shapes. He opened the knife and cut into the cloth, tearing it into strips. Then we cut off the branches to about three-foot lengths.

"You know I really don't know what I'm doing, don't you? I saw this once in a 4-H demonstration." I smiled at Donnie.

"The only thing I can tell you is what I learned from Boy Scouts. I think you are supposed to put the braces on either side of the leg, then wrap around them with a cloth. They should hold the leg from moving and making the break worse. Can you do it?" Donnie raised himself up onto his elbows to watch the procedure.

Donnie held the branches on either side of his leg. Then I began to wrap the cloth strips around the leg and the branches to hold it stiff. Donnie bit his lip to keep from crying out as I moved his leg to wrap the strips around it. Finally, I knotted the end of the last strip.

"I'm no nurse, but that looks pretty good to me. Yuck! The mud! I'm going to see if I can get something to wipe the mud off." I started back down to the creek.

"Sophie, here. Take my sweatshirt," said Donnie, pulling the sweatshirt off over his head and handing it to me.

"You keep that on. It might get cold tonight, and you need something to keep you warm."

I looked down at my bruised and scratched legs and feet, feeling the pain. A little farther along the creek was a sack half-buried in the mud. Inside were some clothes, maybe intended for some garage sale or charity. One article was a tee shirt, which I immediately used to soak up some water from the still rushing creek. I wrung out the excess and carried it back up the embankment to where Donnie was waiting.

"I found something!" I exclaimed, and began to wash off Donnie's face, arms and legs with the cloth. Then I wiped my own face and arms, getting off only the worst of the caked-on mud.

"We need to get you to the shelter I found down the hill. Have you ever slept in a hog shed before?" The whole idea was laughable.

"No, I can't say I have. If you can help me get to my feet, maybe I can hop on one leg." He started to lift himself off the ground, and fell back from the pain in his leg.

"I say we just scoot you down the hill to where I have the hog shed set up. You can use your good foot to help move yourself along, and I'll help you."

Together, we began to move Donnie down the hill toward the hog shed, our shelter from the relentless rain, and quickly slid inside. The remainder of the clothes from the bag was used to dry off arms and legs. The rain had subsided, but continued to patter on the tin roof of the structure. Together we lay on our stomachs in silence, looking out the opening in the shed together, and watching the approach of nightfall.

Chapter 6
DON

The parking lot of the mall was almost empty, except for a few cars randomly parked near store entrances.

"He's probably not even here today," Don said to himself, as he pulled up and parked in front of the art store. He took the business card out of his pocket. Chuck Orman. It was worth a try.

He walked up to the front door of the building. Cupping his hands to look inside, he saw a couple of lights on in the store. He tapped on the glass with his car keys to see if someone would hear him. Just as he was about to turn away from the door, a man wearing a painter's coveralls opened it.

"Can I help you?" the man asked.

"I'm looking for Chuck Orman," Don replied. "Is he here?"

"Step inside, and I'll get him for you." The worker was off to the back of the store.

Don looked around at the shelves and paintings that had been set up in displays. Shelves had already been stocked with painting supplies. Tubes and bottles of paints, brushes, paint thinners and brush cleaners, pallets and drawing utensils, were carefully placed in specific areas of the shelves. Canvases and drawing boards stood stacked and labeled. Easels of every shape and size were set up along one wall. Don felt a kindling of interest, looking at all the familiar items.

"I'm Chuck Orman. How can I help you?" The man was small in stature, but muscular and trim. Don noted that he was dressed for working on the store structure, wearing jeans and a T-shirt and sporting a baseball cap. His brown hair was pulled back into a pony tail at his neckline.

"Glad to meet you, Chuck," said Don, extending his right hand. I'm Don Ribold. A friend of mine, Jerry Cole, told me you were getting ready to open an art shop here, and he suggested I talk to you about getting back into painting."

"Oh, sure, Don. He told me you might stop by. I'm glad you did. Tell me what you have done in the past, and what you'd like to learn."

Don told Chuck about some of his acrylic paintings, emphasizing the fact that he hadn't painted in some time. He only briefly mentioned his early retirement and his wife Arlene, trying to avoid any negativity in their first meeting. He didn't want Chuck to feel pity for him.

"It sounds to me like you already have a good foundation. We might just build on what you already have experience with, and see where it goes from there. When could you come here for classes? I have a couple of them already started. One meets on Monday night at seven, and the other meets on Thursday at six-thirty. I've set up evening classes, as many people work full time and paint as a hobby." Chuck waited for Don's response.

"I can come any time, actually. How about if I come on Monday night? Should I get some supplies ahead of time?"

"Sure, let's take a look at the supply shelves. I'd guess you don't have anything left to work with. Do you still have an easel?" Chuck walked with Don to the shelves of paint supplies.

"I still have an easel, but you're right, no paints or brushes. Whatever you recommend to get started will be fine." Don started looking over the supplies.

Chuck selected a variety of paints, various brushes and some canvas blanks. He handed them to Don as he selected them, Don following him along the aisles in anticipation.

"You are welcome to get started before the class if you like, or you can just wait to paint when you are here. You might be surprised how much you remember." Chuck's eyes were kind and reassuring as he briefly faced Don.

"Thanks, I just might do that. And I'll be ready for Monday night."

"Come prepared to paint while you are here. You will be free to paint whatever you like most of the time. I like to use a hands-on approach to teaching, making suggestions as I observe a painter's work. We will have a great time working together, I'm sure of it." He smiled at Don.

They walked with the supplies to the cash register, set up at the end of a bare counter on one side of the room. "Hopefully we will have this place in better shape by Monday night. So far there are five in the class." Chuck rang up the purchases, and Don paid him.

"I'm really looking forward to it, Chuck," he said, as he gathered up his purchases and walked toward the door. The odor of fresh paint and sawdust wafted through the store, the workers obviously finishing up their work in the back rooms. "Bye for now!"

Don heard the lock turn into the door jamb, as Chuck closed the door behind him. He walked to his car with his treasures and drove back to his condo. The sun was shining through the windows as he entered the room, but he didn't bother to close the drapes. Placing his supplies on the kitchen counter, he hung up his jacket, and started rummaging through closets in search of his easel. After a futile attempt to find it, he thought about the attic above the condo garage. A quick look revealed his lost easel, which he retrieved and brought into the dining room. The legs of the easel seemed a little wobbly, so he tightened the bolts on the braces for stability, and suddenly realized he hadn't felt this enthusiastic for a long time.

He took out one of the blank canvas frames and set it carefully on the easel trough. Could he create as he had long ago? He returned to the garage and retrieved three paintings from the attic, setting them up around the room. "Not too bad, he said to himself, barely remembering the creations.

The acrylics were there on the table, the brushes ready to use, and the pallet empty and waiting for the dollops of paint. Don took a deep breath and sighed.

"No time like the present." He began to squeeze paints into the wells of the pallet. He set the paints and pallet on an oil cloth draped across the dining room table. Then the easel was positioned for a view toward the park on the east side of the building. With a stool retrieved from the kitchen and a bibbed apron covering his shirt and pants, he seated himself in front of the easel. His hand trembled slightly as he picked up a brush from the selection Chuck had recommended. He dabbed it into the water, then the green paint, and began to brush strokes of color onto his easel.

As darkness began to fall across the park, Don realized he had been working for several hours. He felt elated with his progress on the painting, but decided to wash up his brushes and put away the easel for the evening. Maybe, just maybe, he could create some works to hang up in the condo or give to Marty as a gift sometime. The dark clouds that had enveloped him for so long seemed to be clearing slightly as he considered the future.

"Marty, this is Dad." Don spoke into the phone, thinking he might get together with Marty and share his new project.

"Hi, Dad, what are you up to?"

"I just wondered if you had plans for this evening, or if you might want to meet me at the Sports Bar for a steak and a beer. I'll buy." Don was eager to talk to him.

"Well, actually, Janet and the boys are going out to do some shopping, and that would give me a good excuse to not go along. How about if I meet you there around seven?"

"Sounds okay to me. I'll see you then." Don put down the phone and bustled about the condo, cleaning up his work and changing clothes. He smiled when he noted in the mirror that he was whistling as he combed through his snow-white hair. "There was a time when my hair was dark and curly," he said to his image, as though he had to help with the recollection. Then he smiled, the dimples in his cheeks now elongated in the lines of his face.

He flipped off the lights, checked his wallet for cash and credit cards, grabbed his jacket, and was out the door for the evening.

Marty was already at the Sports Bar, watching a game of pool on the television when Don arrived. Don sat across from him in the booth and removed his hat and jacket.

"Hey there! How's it going?" Don enjoyed the atmosphere at the sports bar. It was a place where he and Marty could hang out for a few beers and enjoy the sporting events. Everyone there seemed to be enjoying friends and colleagues.

"Okay, thanks. I ordered a beer, but the waiter will be back to get an order from you in a minute. I wasn't sure what you wanted." Marty reached out to shake hands with his dad.

The waiter arrived with Marty's beer, and took Don's order for a Michelob Light from the tap. "Will you be dining with us tonight as well?"

"Sure thing. Just give us a minute to look over the menu," Don said, opening the menu as he spoke.

"I'll be right back." The waiter was off to the bar.

"Now this is on me tonight, Marty," Don insisted.

"Okay, but what is the occasion? I haven't seen you in such a good mood for a long time." Marty sipped his beer.

Don smiled, knowing Marty was right. "I've signed up for some art lessons and started painting again. I bought some art supplies, and have even found my old easel up in the attic."

"Good God! I can't even remember when I last saw you paint anything. Is it coming back to you?"

"Well, sort of. It's too early to tell yet. I've started working on a scene from the park. The class I'm taking is from Chuck Orman. He's opening a new art shop out at the mall."

The waiter returned with Don's beer, and took out his pencil and order book. "What can I get you?"

Marty and Don gave him their steak dinner orders. Don ordered some calamari for an appetizer. The waiter disappeared through the kitchen doorway.

"I think that's great, Dad. It's so good to see you have an interest in something. By the way, would you want to play a little golf before the weather gets bad? I have a couple of passes to the public golf course from a raffle I entered."

"Sure, just tell me when you want to go. I have lots of time, you know."

"Well, you never know. This painting might just consume all of your free time." Marty winked at him and smiled.

"I always have time for a good game of golf. And I'm not going to let you beat me this time!" Don shook his finger at Marty. He paused for a moment, sipping his beer. "How are things at work?"

"I've been really busy on the civic center project for the city. I still can't believe that Staley is building its own civic center. We almost have all the plans completed and approved. It has really been a humongous project for me."

"Well, I'm proud of you. They couldn't have a better architect working on it. There's no doubt it will be beautiful and functional. Is the city going to stay within budget on it?"

"Pretty much, I'd say. The bonds have been authorized, and we should break ground next month." Marty appeared to be pleased with the outcome of the plans.

They sat silently for a few moments, watching the match of pro pool players on the screen.

"Jesus, did you see that shot!?" Marty exclaimed. "How did he get that ball to just drop into the pocket? Amazing!"

The two of them enjoyed sharing comments on the game, ate their dinners, and left to go their separate ways.

"Dad, now don't get too carried away with all that painting," Marty teased.

"Just don't get too cocky, Marty. You just might see my paintings on display in the civic center someday." Don smiled and turned to walk to his car. He could hardly contain his enthusiasm as he turned the key in the ignition and started toward his condo. This had been the best day for him since Arlene died. No doubt about it. Even the nagging pain in his right leg didn't seem to bother him as much, as he climbed out of the car and walked to his front door. The moon was full, the stars were bright, and the air was crisp with the coming fall weather.

Sophie was so excited about getting back to her writing. Inspired by the journals and her findings in the trunk, she had begun to create her new book, and the writing was going very well. This story would be such a different genre from what she had written before. Three of her previous books had been historical fiction, creating characters from her many travels throughout her life, combined with history of the area dating back to the early settlers in the Midwest. She tried to pull herself away from writing to spend an hour or so in the attic each morning, finishing her coffee, so that she could show Tom she had made some progress.

Tom arrived on Saturday with his pick-up truck. Sophie heated up some caramel rolls, Tom's favorites, and had coffee ready for him.

"You are awesome!" Tom said, giving Sophie a hug.

"Just for my boy," Sophie responded. She poured them a mug of coffee, and sat down with him at the kitchen table.

"So how's the cleaning going?" Tom asked, taking a sip of his coffee.

"When you go up the attic stairs, on the right side there are some boxes for you to take to the dump. There are some old papers there and some other things I don't want to keep any longer."

"Do you have anything that has confidential information on it, like Social Security numbers or check numbers?" Tom asked.

"No, these are just old bookkeeping records. Dad had run all the other stuff through a shredder some time ago. The things up there now are just garbage. Then I have some clothes up there that can go to Good Will. They are in pretty good shape, but no longer in style, especially the coats. Can you take those, too?" Sophie took a roll for herself, tearing off a piece.

"Sure, I'll take anything you want to get rid of. Is there anything I can help you with?"

"No, I need to look at all of it. I don't have much time for this right now, as I'm writing again." Sophie looked at Tom for his response.

"That's okay by me. The girls are the ones who are pushing for you to get to a smaller place. You can stay here as long as you want, as far as I'm concerned." Tom shrugged his shoulders.

"Here I thought you were the one pushing!" Sophie exclaimed. "Shirley was here earlier this week for lunch and she is really anxious for me to get this all done."

"Well, you just do what you want to do, Mom. If you want to spend all your time writing, then that's what you should do. Just tell Shirley and Trudy to buzz off!"

"They mean well. They are concerned about me with Dad gone now, and have forgotten that I can still do things for myself. It will all work out." Sophie appreciated Tom's support. "I might just see how much the house would bring, if I were to put it up for sale, and how much work would need to be done."

"If there are some minor repairs, I can do those for you. But if there are major things, then you will have to hire someone. I just don't have the time." Tom turned his attention to the breakfast rolls. "Yum, these are delicious!"

"The house could probably use some painting in some of the rooms and maybe some new carpet. The family room is really worn. What would you suggest?" Sophie ran her fingers back through her thick, greying hair to push it back from her face.

"If you talk to a realtor, you will find out what is recommended to sell a house and how much difference it might make in your price. It's worth a shot. Do you still want to have the garden space?"

"I do. That's the hardest part of giving up this house. I have so much time invested in the yard and gardens. And I love to work out there. There's no doubt the house will be lonely this winter without your dad." Sophie looked out the window toward the back yard.

"Sure it will. But if you bake these rolls for me, I'll be sure to come for a visit!" Tom kissed her on the cheek, and got up to pour another cup of coffee. "So, what are you writing about?"

"I ran across some old journals I had kept as a child, and decided to create a story from them. The journals are from when I was about ten until about fourteen. It's been kind of fun, but I don't want to give it all away." Sophie teased Tom, determined to keep her story a secret for now.

"So this is story about you? Well, good luck with that. Do you still keep in touch with your agent?"

"Yes, but I'll have to send her a note to let her know about this book. I haven't sent her anything for so long, since I was taking care of your dad. She'll be surprised to hear from me, especially when I give her the details of the story."

"Maybe this will be your number one best seller! It will be all about my favorite heroine." Tom raised his coffee cup in a toast.

Sophie laughed at him. "Right!"

Tom opened the door to the attic stairs and climbed up into the attic to retrieve the boxes and clothes, making several trips out to his truck with them. Sophie made sure he knew which ones were to go to the dump, and which ones were for Good Will. They talked about the Christmas decorations, and she gave him a bag of pictures of his family. Then he went on his way to deliver the contents of his truck.

Sophie spent a little time in the attic, rearranging some things with the additional space. She even now had an area where she could do some sorting. But her mind wasn't on this kind of work. She returned to her writing.

Chapter 8

THE STORY CONTINUES

The rain had slowed to a sprinkle and all the ground around the small shelter was completely saturated with water. Donnie and I lay side by side on the ground and looked out the opening. We could hear the water in the creek still moving in torrents on the other side of the knoll from where we had set up our shelter. We were wet and chilled from the dampness. Drying as much as we could with the clothes found in the small bag, we had wiped away some of the mud that was caked to our bodies.

Donnie was in pain with his broken leg. "Sophie, we have to get some help. My leg hurts bad."

I looked down at his leg, and then looked into his eyes. I could see the pain reflected in them. "I'm not sure if I should leave you to try to get some help, or if we should stay here. What do you think?"

"You might take a look around to see what you can see. I should be okay here until you can get some help."

Crawling out of the shelter, and glancing back at Donnie, I climbed up the knoll, slipping on the wet grass and mud. I looked out in all directions, trying to see how far the water in the creek might have carried us. Nothing looked familiar. The sun was about to drop behind the horizon, and it would be dark soon. A shiver went through me at the thought of spending the night in the small shelter, cold and wet from the persistent rain.

To the east and across the creek water, a farm house loomed in the distance. But it wouldn't be safe to try to cross the creek to get there. To the northwest, I could see a barn, but didn't know if there was a house on the farmstead. Turning to look to the southwest, I could see a house and farm buildings in the distance. I could probably make it there before dark, if I ran across the pasture.

I climbed back down to the shelter and Donnie. "I can see a house off to the southwest, and can probably make it there before dark. Will you be all right here if I go?"

"How far is it? Will you be okay?" Donnie was more concerned about me.

"I think so. If I can get to the farmhouse, I should be able to call home for some help. Then we can get you to a doctor. They have to be looking for us by now, don't you think?" I was apprehensive about leaving for the farmhouse.

"Yeah, I'm sure they must be. I just hope everyone is okay."

Without another word, I started out to the southwest, keeping the farmhouse in my sights, and sloshing through the mud and water as I made my way into the field. My feet were bare, and the stubble of the grasses poked sore and swollen feet. I tried to watch where I was stepping, avoiding any cow piles or holes in the ground. I wondered briefly if there might be any animals awaiting me near the barn. Finally, I reached the outbuildings and made my way across the yard to the house. There was no activity anywhere outside.

As I stepped onto the porch, I noticed that the paint was worn and the banisters were splintered. A cat jumped out and ran away into the barnyard. There were no lights on in the house, and it was nearly dark outside. Approaching the door cautiously, I looked to the sides and behind me as I reached up to ring the doorbell. Nothing happened; no sound from inside to indicate the doorbell was working. I knocked on the door as hard as I could, and waited for a response. No one came to the door. The darkness was enveloping me, and I felt panic rising in my throat.

Suddenly an unusual light came on in the barn, streaming out into the barnyard. I walked carefully down from the porch and made my way toward the light, my heart racing. I reached the doorway and looked into the barn. An older man was moving some hay from a stack of bales into the feeder for the cattle. He had not yet seen me.

"Hello?" I called out, expecting the man to be startled by my voice. I was not disappointed. The man reeled around with his pitchfork to look toward the sound of my voice.

"Hello, my name is Sophie Palmer. Can you help me?" I shivered, knowing that I must look like a waif, covered with blood and mud as I was.

"What are you doing here?" the man asked.

"My friend and I got caught up by the storm, and were washed down the creek. He has a broken leg, and I came here to get some help. Can you help us?" Tears were stinging my eyes, all strength and resolve now gone.

"Come sit down here on the bales, and let's have a look at you," the farmer said, as he motioned to me to come into the barn. "Where is your friend?"

I made my way across the barn floor toward the bales of hay and sat down gingerly, tears streaming down my cheeks.

"He's back by the creek under the roof of a hog house for shelter. I left him there to get some help. He's in a lot of pain. We made him a brace for his leg, but we are both soaking wet and cold." I couldn't stop the words or the tears at this point.

"Let's take you up to the house and get you dry. Then we can go find your friend. My name's Joe. Joe Dixon. I live here alone." He took my hand and led me across the barn floor, through the barnyard, and toward the back door of the house. "Where're your kinfolk?"

"I don't know where I am, or how far we came down the creek. My dad is Jim Palmer, and my friend is staying with his aunt and uncle, Jack Ribold." I was following along with Joe, feeling assured of his help. "They are probably looking for us. Do you have a phone so we can call them?"

"The phones are out from the storm. But we'll get your friend back here and you can get warm and cleaned up." Joe smiled at me reassuringly, alleviating my fears.

Inside the kitchen, it was easy to tell that Joe was not a good housekeeper. There were pans and dirty dishes stacked up by the sink. The table was covered with papers and magazines and coffee cups. Cupboard doors stood open, their contents set up precariously inside. A box of sugar had tipped over, spilling some of its contents onto a shelf below and the counter. The stove was thick with cooking grease burned onto the burners. Joe motioned for me to sit down on a kitchen chair.

"Sit down here, little lady. I'll get you a blanket to wrap up in." Joe moved some papers off the table and stacked them on top the garbage can. He carried cups to the sink and then disappeared through a doorway on the other side of the kitchen. When he returned, he had a blanket and a pail of warm water with a washcloth. "Why don't you wash up a little, and then you can show me where to find your friend."

I picked out the wash cloth, wrung it out, and washed off my face and arms. The warm water helped to stop the crying, and I felt better just to get a little of the drying mud off my legs. I dried off with the small hand towel Joe had brought. The blanket felt good around my shoulders. Then my thoughts returned to Donnie, in the cold dampness of the night.

"We need to get Donnie," I urged, anxious for Donnie, lying in the darkness.

"Okay, if you're ready. We can take the tractor and the cart and drive across the field. That way we will have light and a way to bring your friend back here." Joe started out the back door of the kitchen with me close at his heels.

We returned to the barn, where Joe started a small tractor and hooked a two-wheeled cart to the hitch. I climbed up with him onto the tractor, and we turned out of the barn toward where I had left Donnie. The tractor lurched and spun its tires through the muddy field as Joe guided it in the direction I indicated. In a few moments, we reached the small shelter.

"Donnie! We're here to help you!" I shouted as I jumped down from the tractor and ran to Donnie. Joe followed me to my injured friend.

"Hi, Donnie. I'm Joe. I'll get this hog shed off you and then I can lift you up onto the cart. Hang on there, fella." Joe was reassuring to Donnie.

"I am so glad to see you! It was so dark and spooky out here all alone."

"I'll bet it was. You just hang on now, and we'll get you back to my place where you can get warmed up." Joe lifted the roof structure and tipped it over. Then he reached down and picked up Donnie to put him into the cart. I climbed onto the cart with Donnie to make sure he didn't slide off the end as we made our way back across the field.

Back at Joe's place, we got Donnie inside the house and placed him on an old day bed in what appeared to be a den in the house. I had thrown a blanket over the day bed cover, as Donnie was covered in mud.

"We need to get those clothes off of you and get you washed up. It looks like you have a pretty good splint there on your leg. I have some stuff you can put on. It'll be way too big for you, but at least we can get you dry. Sophie, if you want to wait in the kitchen, I'll help Donnie get a little more comfortable. Then we'll wrap up his leg and think about how we are going to get him some help." Joe had taken charge of the situation.

I went back out to the kitchen. Finding some dish soap, I ran some water in the sink to wash up some dishes. The water felt warm and comforting on my hands and arms. I stacked the dishes as I rinsed them. After wiping off the counter, I sat down in the chair and felt the fatigue from the events of the day begin to take hold. I was startled to hear Joe announce that I could come in to see Donnie, as I had drifted off to sleep momentarily.

"Hey, I'll just have to keep you here! Thanks for cleaning up the kitchen. Listen, I need to go out to finish the chores. You two kids keep dry in here, and I'll be back in shortly." Joe tipped his hat to Sophie, and left through the back door to return to the barn.

Chapter 9

ART LESSONS FOR DON

Don made his way across the parking lot at the mall toward Chuck Orman's art shop. He had a fresh canvas and a small carrier with his supplies in hand. A young man greeted him as he entered the shop.

"Welcome. My name is Tom. Are you new to the art class?"

"Yes, this is my first time. I'm looking forward to it," Don replied.

"You can go on into the back room and set up there before we get started," Tom suggested. "Hang up your jacket back there on the coat tree."

"Thanks." Don walked through the store to the back room, now freshly painted by the workers he had seen on his earlier visit. He saw that there were some easels set up with accompanying stools, and found a spot near the front to assemble his supplies. After removing his jacket, he got a cup of coffee from the table set up for refreshments and awaited the start of the class.

Don counted five additional students as they joined him in the classroom, all younger than he and dressed in very casual jeans and tennis shoes. He felt out of place and over-the-hill in comparison, that is until Chuck Orman joined them.

"Class, meet Don Ribold. Don has had a good deal of experience in acrylic painting, but wants to work with us here to get back in practice. Don, can you tell us a little about yourself?"

Don felt much better already, with that introduction. "As Chuck says, I used to do a good deal of painting, but haven't touched a brush for some time. I'm hoping you folks can help me get back into the swing of things. I've spent a number of years in the insurance business, am now retired and a widower, and I need projects or a hobby to keep me busy."

"Welcome, Don!" one of the students said. The others chimed in with brief introductions. Don hoped he could remember the names. He used to practice a method for name recognition, and recalled this as each of the students talked. Backgrounds and interests varied, but all were eager to learn and enhance their skills.

"Class, as you know, I like to be hands on when I am teaching, so I've set up a group of objects here on the table I would like for you to paint. I realize that some of you may be more skilled at landscapes than at still life painting, but I want to get a better sense of your own personal style. So let's get started this evening. Does everyone have all the supplies we need? As you know, I have plenty of supplies in the shop!" Chuck grinned as he gestured toward the front of the store.

The class responded with a collective sigh. One commented, "Okay, Chuck. Always the salesman!"

Don selected the colors he wanted to use for the painting and set them up on his pallet. Using a wide brush with broad strokes, he started with the background colors, his hand feeling totally in control as though he had been painting for many years.

"Nice strokes on that color, Don. You might want to consider highlighting and contrasting to get more depth in the texture of your paint. Just a suggestion." Chuck studied the painting, his hand cupped under his chin. He patted Don on the shoulder and continued on to the next student.

"Sure, why didn't I think of that?" Don thought to himself. "But that's what I'm here for!" He smiled as he dabbled in some lighter and darker colors in the appropriate places on the canvas.

After about twenty minutes, Chuck called their attention to the still life. "Ladies and gentlemen, I want you to take a careful look at these items. Note that these are not just inanimate objects. You can see life in them, if you look at what they reflect. You can see the lights from the ceiling in this vase. You can see various stages of blooms in the flowers. It is very important to capture all of this for the viewer, or your painting is dull and lifeless. Let's take a break for a few moments. You can get a cup of coffee or some hot tea in the back, and I think there are a few cookies out there as well."

Don wrapped his brush in a piece of plastic, wiped off his hands on his apron, and got up from his stool. The young man next to him walked over toward him.

"Nice job, Don. Clayton Jones. You have a really nice touch with this. What genre do you prefer for your paintings?"

"Thanks, Clayton." Don extended his hand in greeting. "I really prefer landscapes. I find it much more interesting to capture nature on the canvas. There is so much variety and opportunity for color and impression. What about you?"

"I prefer landscapes as well. I've done a lot with city buildings and local parks, but have never tried to do anything in the country. Come on back, and I'll buy you a cup of coffee." Clayton laughed as he laid his hand on Don's shoulder. Don liked this young man.

The students all shared a few ideas about the still life, as well as a few light hearted jokes, until Chuck called them all back to the task at hand. With a few more tips from Chuck, Don was totally lost in his creation. His hands moved swiftly, using a variety of brush strokes, colors and hues in his impressions of the subject. He felt totally at peace and excited about his work. The young people around him seemed to accept him as a fellow student, and he enjoyed their input.

"Okay, everyone. We are going to call it a night. You are welcome to leave your canvases here, but you will need to set them off the easel and onto the tables in the back. I'll need these for the next class. Next week, I'm going to bring in another subject. You can finish up the one you are working on and begin on the next one. I think you will find the new one more challenging than this one was for you. By the way, there is a contest coming up here in town at the college art center. I'd like to see all of you enter something in this, even if you don't think your work is of the highest quality. You never know what the judges will be looking for. It's just two weeks from this weekend, so be thinking about what you would like to enter. We'll fill out the forms next week in class. The fee is only ten dollars to enter. See you all next week?" Chuck started to gather up his papers from his podium.

"Chuck, do you think we are ready for a contest?" Don asked, cleaning his brushes, and capping his paint supplies.

"Don and everyone, working toward entering a contest will motivate you to do your best work. And, as I said, you never know what the judges will be looking for. I think everyone in this room has a chance." He smiled at Don's misgivings.

All the students were quiet as they cleaned up their area and carried their canvases to the back of the room, propping them against the back wall. The challenge was issued. Each of them would have to practice over the week ahead and give some thought as to what to enter.

"Clayton, I guess we will have to just do the best we can, right?" Don asked his new friend as they left the building together.

"Please call me 'Clay'. And you are right. The challenge is made; the die is cast!" He gestured with a flare of his arms and grinned at his own dramatics. "Besides, you will probably win, hands down!"

"Oh, please. I'm so rusty. But I'm enjoying every minute of this class. I'll see you next week, Clay?"

"See you then!" Clay pulled out his car keys and walked to his car, while Don strolled on down the row to his own vehicle.

Back at the condo, Don collapsed into his recliner and clicked on the television. He was tired, but felt alive and revitalized. There must be something around the condo to make a good subject for a contest piece. His eyes wandered around the living room in search of an appropriate subject, but he didn't find anything that fit the bill. Tomorrow he would decide on what to enter in the contest.

It was still dark when Don awoke. He had trouble sleeping with the visions of his still life haunting his dreams. The colors and the objects became blurred and ran together. He washed his face in the bathroom, dressed and grabbed his morning meds, and headed down the street toward the diner for breakfast. Dawn was just breaking when he arrived.

"Good grief, what brings you in here at this hour?" asked Suzy, as she looked up to see him come in the door.

"Just don't give me a hard time, will you? I couldn't sleep last night, so I just decided to get up and eat some breakfast. I have things to do today!" Don hung his hat on the hat tree and strolled to his usual booth.

"Well, what's gotten into you? I haven't seen you in this good a mood for a coon's age!" Suzy exclaimed. "And it's only six-thirty in the morning!" she teased.

"Just pour the coffee," Don smiled. "I'll have some OJ and some biscuits and gravy, if you please. And be quick about it!" He clapped his hands and grinned at her.

"You better smile when you say that," she warned him as she poured his coffee into a mug on the table. She took out her order pad and jotted down Don's order. "Lord, it's going to rain today for sure!" she muttered as she walked to the order window and posted her note.

Don picked up the newspaper from the counter and glanced through the front page. On the second page, he noted an article about the civic center and Marty's name was mentioned as the architect on the project. He felt a sense of pride in Marty's ability. He looked up and out the window, thinking of Marty's challenges after college, and how he had helped Marty get through rehab following Annie's death.

"That reminds me, I need to get over to Green Meadow and visit the graves," he thought to himself. Don's daughter, Annie, and Arlene were both buried at the Green Meadow cemetery. Don and Arlene had raised the kids in Green Meadow, but moved to Staley after Annie died so that Arlene would be closer to her work at the Mill.

He read the funnies and the sports section. In the local news he saw the notice of the art contest at the college. Who would have ever thought he might be entering a contest in art at this age? Arlene would think he had lost his mind.

Suzy brought his orange juice and his breakfast and had refilled his coffee mug. He was hungry, and wolfed down his breakfast, setting his plate aside for Suzy to pick up on her way through the diner. He held his coffee mug with both hands, staring out the window and considering possibilities for his art project.

"The old farm, that's it!" Don said out loud, suddenly realizing that others had heard his comment. "Sorry, just thinking," he said to the couple in the next booth, blushing slightly. But he had the idea. He hadn't been to Illinois and the farm, where he used to visit his aunt and uncle when he was very young, for many years. It would be the perfect spot for a landscape painting for the contest. It was early enough that he could make the drive today, and the weather was going to be clear and sunny. He could stop by the cemetery in Green Meadow on his way. Don slid quickly out of his booth, stopping by the cash register on his way out the door to pay for his breakfast.

"I didn't even have time to total your ticket, Don!" said Suzy, as she completed the ticket and took his money. "You have yourself a great day."

"You, too, Suzy. I'll probably see you tomorrow!"

Don walked quickly back to his condo, passing the stores along his route, still closed in the early morning hour. The birds seemed to be singing particularly loud this morning. He grabbed the painting supplies he had left out on the kitchen counter after last night's class. Armed with his easel and a couple of fresh canvases, he deposited them in the back seat of his car along with the paints he thought would become a part of the painting.

He stopped at the Quick-Stop on the corner to pick up a couple of bouquets of fresh flowers for the grave flower stands at the cemetery. Traffic in Staley was never very heavy, and Don was on his way out of town in a matter of minutes. Green Meadow was right off the highway from Staley, about forty-five minutes east. He found WLS Talk Radio on his AM dial, and settled into his drive.

At the cemetery, Don made his way to the graves of his wife and daughter. After placing the flowers in each of the urns beside the headstones, he sat down on a nearby bench.

"Arlene, I can't tell you how excited I am. You remember how much I enjoyed painting when we were first married? You used to scold me for spending so much time in the spare bedroom painting, rather than spending time with you. Well, I'm taking a class and painting again. I've been so lonely and depressed, and am really excited about meeting some people who share my interests. My classmates and I are going to enter a contest in a couple of weeks." He paused for a moment. "Miss you, honey," he said, a catch in his voice. He rose from the bench, walked to Arlene's headstone and rearranged the flowers there, then walked back to his car. For the first time, he felt it was going to be okay to move on with his life.

The drive to Central Illinois took him another two hours, and he arrived at a local café in Clarion not far from his Uncle Jack's farm. He noted that the trees around the café were several brilliant colors of autumn, perfect for his paintings. Judy's Café was not particularly busy, as it was just eleven-thirty. He walked to a vinyl-covered booth toward the back and picked up the menu from the stand behind the salt and pepper shakers and condiments. The menu consisted of two typed sheets in a plastic binder, featuring breakfast on one side and sandwiches on the other. A waitress brought him a glass of ice water and his utensils, wrapped tightly in a napkin.

Don ordered his meal and settled back to take in the café. An L-shaped counter with chrome stools was occupied by a number of locals, dressed in work clothes. There were several framed quotes and jokes for the benefit of the patrons. There was also a large round table with a group of men in conversation. Don assumed them to be farmers in the area.

After his quick lunch, he drove to the edge of town, trying to remember how to get to the farm from there. If his memory served him right, he would drive north about two miles, and then take a road to the east. Surely he would recognize buildings on the farm when he got close. He drove across a wooden plank bridge above a creek, and his heart jumped to think he was close to his destination. Suddenly, off to the right, he could see a familiar red barn, a large white two-story house, and a tree-lined lane that looked familiar. It was Uncle Jack's farm, for sure. Beyond the farm buildings, he could see the fields and the timber that ran along the creek. This had to be the place. Don wondered who might be living here now, as Uncle Jack had sold the farm. He had been dead for many years. Don drove slowly up the driveway to the house, and parked his car at the end of the sidewalk.

Although many things looked familiar, there were newer buildings, and the house and barn seemed smaller than he remembered them to be. The trees in the yard were beautiful in their vibrant colors of fall, enhanced by the sunshine that had blessed his day. It seemed strange to be here in this place, so familiar yet different.

Don walked up onto the porch by the back door, and knocked on the screen door. A lovely woman came to the door, wiping her hands on an apron.

"Hello, can I help you?" she asked, her eyes scanning the stranger before her, as well as his car.

"I hope so. My name is Don Ribold, and I used to come here to this farm to visit my Uncle Jack and Aunt Edna when I was a boy."

"Hello, Don," the woman extended her hand. "I'm Janice Griffin. My father-in-law bought this farm from Jack Ribold many years ago, and my husband farms the ground."

"I'm doing some painting, and I wondered if you would mind if I walk back into the timber and set up my easel for a time this afternoon?" Don gestured toward the timber behind the farm.

"Well, I guess that would be all right," she responded. "Do you know your way back there?"

"I think I can remember. Is it okay if I leave my car here in the driveway?"

"Sure, that would be fine. When you get ready to leave, why don't you stop back by the house to tell us you are leaving?" Janice's request was more of an order, Don assumed her to be just a little uncomfortable with his presence there.

"I'll do that. It will probably be several hours. I want to capture the sun in a couple of different angles and lights. Thank you," Don started back toward his car to retrieve his supplies. His heart was racing at the prospect of returning to this place. He wanted to go inside the barn to look around, but thought Janice might be nervous with any further investigating. The open doorway revealed a large harvesting vehicle. He looked back and noted that Janice was still watching him, so he decided to settle for his walk to the timber.

As he neared the trees along the creek, he wondered if his perspective would be better in the field as opposed to inside the cover of the trees. He decided to go on into the shaded area to take a look around first. He found his way through the tall oaks and the hedge trees, finally reaching the creek running peacefully through the creek bed. The small walk bridge was still there, maybe thirty yards away from where he had entered the grove. Still clutching his easel and his supplies, he walked carefully across the bridge, noting some rotting boards that were not too dependable. He marveled again at his perception of the size of this bridge as he remembered it. On the opposite bank, he walked several yards into the trees, trying to remember where he had first found Sophie Palmer in that little hut she and her brother had constructed. He smiled to himself, thinking of Sophie and wondering where she might be now. The last summer he had spent with his aunt and uncle had been such a special time for him, filled with memories.

Looking through the trees, he noted Sophie's farm. Using that as a guide, found his way to the area where the hide-out had once been built. To his surprise, some of the branches and boards they had used were still there. He noted something shiny under some of the logs, and removed them one by one to get to it. It was a thermos bottle, perhaps once filled with iced tea.

Don looked up to see the sun shining on the side of the barn on Sophie's parents' farm. The trees surrounding it were vibrant with gold and reds of fall, and it would be a perfect setting for a landscape. He quickly set up his easel and selected his paints to squeeze out onto his pallet. His pulse was racing, and he felt totally caught up in the work before him. His brushes flew in capturing the moment and the autumn landscape before him. It was as though someone else was moving his fingers and hands in cadence with the crickets and cicadas among the trees of the timber. Behind him the water trickled and murmured as it moved slowly among the rocks and boulders.

Suddenly, he was startled by a noise not far to his left. He glanced around quickly to see what it was and where it was coming from. A small black and white kitten made its way toward him, mewing hungrily.

"Well, hi, little fella," Don said, as he reached for the small animal. "What are you doing out here all by yourself?" He looked around for any sign of a mother cat, or another person who might have joined him in his sanctuary, but there were no signs of life. The kitten purred as he held it, rubbing its face against his chest. "You are a cute one," he said aloud. "I'll have to take you back to the house with me to see if Janice knows where you belong." He set the kitten down inside his hat, where it stretched and fell quickly asleep.

Don continued with his painting, standing back occasionally to see what he had accomplished. He was pleased with the outcome. But the sun was starting to decline in the west, leaving him with little time to complete more than one painting. With any luck the Griffins would allow him to return.

Don gathered up his supplies, his painting, and his little stray friend, and walked back across the bridge and across the field to the Griffin house. There he put his supplies in the car, careful to lay out the painting in the trunk, and carried the small kitten to the house with him.

"Looks like you have found a friend," said Janice as she answered the door.

"Well, she found me, actually, out in the timber. Do you know who she belongs to by any chance? She is definitely not afraid of people." Don looked to Janice for resolution.

"No, it's hard to say. If you'd like to take her along with you, you are welcome to do so. I have some cat food and a little milk we could give her."

"Now what would I do with a cat?"

"Well, Don, you just set up a little cat box in your house, and feed her, and she will pretty much take care of herself." Janice smiled, knowing that Don really didn't need for her to tell him how to take care of a cat. She walked back into the house to retrieve a small dish of milk and a small bag with some cat food and handed them to Don. "Here you go."

"Janice, do you mind if I come back sometime? There is some really great scenery from back in the timber by the creek, and I'd like to do more painting there." Don was pretty sure she would agree.

"You are welcome to come back any time. If you want, you can just park your car back by the chicken shed over there, and walk back into the timber. I'll tell Lloyd about you, so he will know whose car is here, and maybe you'll get to meet him sometime." Janice walked out onto the porch to assure Don he was welcome.

"Thank you. I'll be back!" Don said as returned to his car with his new friend. He put his hat down on the passenger seat and placed the kitten inside. The long fingers of shadows in the late afternoon sun stretched across the driveway as Don drove back out to the blacktop to begin his trek back to Iowa. "I have no idea what to call you," he said to the little black and white ball of fur. "How about Hope. That's it: Hope. Today has given me hope for tomorrow." He laughed as Hope stretched and rolled back up to go to sleep inside his hat.

Chapter 10

SOPHIE AND DONNIE, 1954

Sophie Writes

I walked into the den where Donnie lay on the day bed, his leg wrapped in some gauze and propped up on a pillow. Joe had found some shorts and a clean shirt for him, and had washed off most of the mud. His hair was combed back from his face.

"Nice hairdo!" I teased, as I walked toward him.

"Thanks. Say, what do you make of this guy? He's kind of weird, don't you think?" Donnie's face showed his concern.

"Kind of. The house is a mess, but if he's a bachelor, that makes some sense. He said he has chores to do, but I didn't see any animals around out there." I peered out the window toward the barn. The door was slightly ajar, allowing a beam of light to shine through the opening. "Maybe I should check it out."

"You stay right here. You might get yourself into trouble. In any case, how are we going to get word to my aunt and uncle and your folks, if the phone lines are down? I need to get to a hospital to get this leg set and cast." Donnie was still in pain from his injury.

"Joe said he'd be right back, so maybe he'll take us home. He just seemed to be really preoccupied with what he was doing in the barn." I turned briefly to talk to Donnie, and then looked back out toward the barn. Donnie was startled to see me duck down below the window sill.

"What happened?" Donnie asked, trying to see out the window from his bed.

"Two guys just walked into the barn. I couldn't see where they came from. We need to turn out that light!" I crawled across the room on hands and knees and turned the knob on the light stand, leaving the room in darkness. Then I crawled back toward the window and looked out from the side of the frame.

Light poured out through the open door from the naked bulb hanging from the beam in the barn. I saw one of the men holding a gun, aiming it at Joe, while the other man was shouting at him. I couldn't make out what they were saying.

"I'm scared, Donnie. One of the men has a gun aimed at Joe. They are yelling at him." I continued to look out from my hidden position by the side of the window. Suddenly, the door of the barn swung wide open, and Joe came out first with his hands in the air. He stumbled slightly, as the man with the gun shoved him forward.

"They are coming this way!" I exclaimed to Donnie. "We need to hide."

I grabbed Donnie by the back of his arms and pulled him down toward the floor. He cried out in pain as his heel thumped against the floor in front of the bed. Then I pushed him under the bed all the way to the wall, and climbed under after him, pulling the blanket to hang down to the floor in front of the bed. I was trembling and breathing hard. "Just be quiet. I think they are coming into the house."

We heard the kitchen door slam open against the wall, and the three men entered the room. "Just sit your ass down in that chair!" one of them yelled.

I scooted back closer to Donnie. He put one arm around me and pulled me close to him, the both of us trembling with fear.

"I told you I don't have much here at the house," Joe said.

"Well, let's see just what you have then. Jake, see what's in the other rooms. Where will we find your money?" The same voice as before was giving the orders.

"In my bedroom, in the top drawer on the right side of the dresser. There are some bills in there. I just don't keep much money here at the house." Joe's voice was steady.

A light came on in the den, and one of the men walked around the room, then walked down the hall toward the bedrooms. We lay perfectly still, almost afraid to breath.

"Well, maybe we will have to take a little ride into town, so you can get some money for us. Got your checkbook handy?" Again, the same voice.

"I have it. There isn't a lot of money in my account at all. I haven't sold my grain yet, so don't have much money in the account. But you are welcome to whatever is in there. The grocery store will still be open, and I can write a check there for cash."

Footsteps echoed from the hallway, across the den and into the kitchen. "Look what I found, Charlie! A couple of real nice guns!" Jake had returned with his find.

"Did you find the money?" Charlie asked.

"Yup! It was just like he said, in the dresser."

"How much is it?"

The voices were quiet for a moment, as Jake counted the money from the dresser.

"Looks like three hundred dollars. These here guns is worth a lot more than that!" The man called Jake was pleased with his discovery.

Charlie expressed his displeasure with the amount of the money they had found. "Well, that just isn't enough money for us, Mister. We are going to have to take you for a little ride. Anyone else live here?"

"Nope. I live here alone. I was just finishing up some chores in the barn, and I've been outside most of the day." Joe was being honest with his captors.

"You do the dishes?" Charlie asked.

"Yeah, I just grabbed a bite to eat about an hour ago, and the place was such a mess." Joe's voice remained calm.

Jake was getting edgy. "Let's go, Charlie. I want to get the money and get out of here."

"I could have sworn I saw someone in here earlier. This light in the den was on." Charlie walked to the doorway of the den and flipped on the switch.

Joe stood up from his chair, and Sophie could see the shadows. "You must have seen the kitchen light. I always turn all the lights off when I'm outside. I'm too poor to pay those high electric bills!" He flipped off the light in the den.

"Okay. Let's go. We'll take your truck, Mister. Jake and me came on foot." Charlie pushed Joe toward the kitchen door. The three men left the house and slammed the door shut behind them.

We lay perfectly still, breathing only slightly. Outside we heard the engine of Joe's truck come to life, and heard the crunching of the gravel as the truck turned into the lane. Then it stopped. I knew they were looking back at the house to see if any lights came on. We still could not move. Finally, after several minutes had passed, the sound of the crunching gravel could be heard as the truck moved on down the gravel lane toward the highway. I inched out from under the bed, my eyes adjusting to the darkness of the room.

Just as I was approaching the window, I heard the truck on the gravel again. Quick as lightening, I slid back under the bed, just as the kitchen door flew open.

"Forgot the damn guns!" the man named Jake exclaimed, as he picked up the guns and again left the house.

My heart was beating so hard, I thought the intruder surely could have heard it when he came in. This time the truck spun out in the gravel and made its way down the driveway, squealing tires as it pulled onto the highway.

Again I crept out from under the bed and looked out the window from the side of the frame. There was no one in sight, and the darkness enveloped us.

I reached under the bed to grab Donnie's hand. "Donnie, what are we going to do? What if they come back here? What if they hurt Joe? I'm so scared!" I pulled Donnie out and collapsed against the chair across the room, and could not stop the tears.

"We've got to get somewhere to get some help for Joe. Those guys were pretty desperate. Once he gets to town with them and gets them some money, it's hard to say what will happen!" Donnie sat up and leaned against the bed.

We sat silently in the darkness for a few minutes, both of our minds racing to figure out what to do, and how to manage an escape.

"I can't leave you here, Donnie, or I could make a run for it. I'm afraid they'll either come back here, or they will do something awful to Joe!" I whispered to Donnie, as though I could be overheard in the darkness.

Donnie reached out for my hand. "Do you think you could drive the tractor?"

"Drive the tractor? Are you crazy? I have never driven anything before, and I have no idea how to start it or stop it." I could not comprehend Donnie's idea.

"But you were on the tractor with Joe. Did you see how he started it? I'd bet you can steer it. If you can, we can get me onto the tractor, and try to get to the next house down the road."

"Donnie, that's the craziest idea I've ever heard. What if I drove it in the ditch or something?"

"Maybe I could stand on the hitch or the wheel well and help you guide it. I've driven my uncle's tractor, and I could coach you." Donnie tried to be convincing.

"How are we going to get you out of the house and on to the tractor, I'd like to know?"

"If you can help me get up on my good leg and give me a shoulder to lean on, I can hop out the door. Joe left the tractor and wagon parked at the end of the sidewalk. We'll figure it out when we get there."

"Well, we can't stay here, that's for sure. It's hard to say how far they have already gotten with Joe. We have to get to someone who can help us." I stood up to look out the window. "It's really dark out there."

Donnie braced himself against the bed, and helped me lift him to stand on his good leg. He said his right leg was throbbing with pain from the sudden blood flow. He put an arm around my shoulders, and I looped an arm around his waist. With Donnie hopping on one leg, we moved to the kitchen door. I opened the door, switched on an outside light, and maneuvered Donnie out onto the stoop. Carefully, we made it to the sidewalk leading to the tractor. When we got to the tractor, Donnie reached up to grab the seat with both hands to pull himself up onto the axle cover. He leaned against the fender skirts. I climbed into the seat and looked down at the gauges and handles.

"I have no clue what to do here, Donnie. It's hard to see anything!"

"Can you reach the pedals?" he asked.

I stretched out my legs. "Yeah, I can reach them if I sit on the very edge of the seat."

"Okay. Here's what you need to do. The pedal on the left is the clutch, and the one on the right is the brake. You need to push the clutch in first. Then you turn the key to start the tractor. When you get it started, you have to put the gear shift all the way to the left and push up. Then let up very slowly on the clutch, and the tractor will start moving. If you let it up too fast, you'll kill the engine and have to start over again. Are you ready?" Donnie was trying to be patient with his instructions.

I pushed the clutch to the floor of the tractor. As I turned the key, the engine fired and engaged. Sitting on the very edge of the tractor seat to hold in the clutch, I pulled the gear shift to the left and pushed up on it, locking into first gear. Then I let up slowly on the clutch.

Suddenly the tractor started to move. I was startled and jerked my foot off the clutch to catch my balance. The tractor lurched forward and jerked ahead, bucking like a horse, and almost throwing Donnie off his perch. In a few seconds, the movement smoothed out, and we crept along slowly

Donnie grabbed the steering wheel to help me get the wheels headed down the driveway toward the road ahead. "Hang on, Sophie. We are going to do this together! Pull out the button on the dash for some light."

I pulled out the button, and the driveway came to life in front of us. The road was just a few yards away. "Oh, Donnie, I don't know if I can do this!" I exclaimed, taking over the steering wheel.

"When you get to the road, let the front wheels get out a little ways onto the road, and then turn the wheel slowly to the right. We need to make sure we don't dump the trailer into the ditch. Don't worry about the clutch or the brake for right now, okay?"

"Okay." I held onto the steering wheel as though it were my lifeline in a sea of water. When we got to the road, I turned the steering wheel to the right, and swung the tractor and trailer onto the road. The right wheel of the trailer dipped only slightly into the edge of the ditch as I turned.

"Great job!" Donnie was excited at the progress. "Let's just creep along at this speed for now. I don't know how far it is to the next place, but at least we are moving. If you get really brave, we can shift into a higher gear."

"Oh, no, thank you. This is as fast as I want to go for now." I was gripping the steering wheel, my knuckles white.

"Now, if we have to stop, you will need to push in the clutch first, then the brake. You should be able to stop the tractor with no problem."

We crept along the blacktopped road at a snail's pace, scanning the horizon for any sign of lights. As we reached the top of a hill, we could see what appeared to be a house on the left side of the road, about half a mile away, and at the end of a long lane.

Chapter 11
SOPHIE

"Hello, Angie? This is Sophie Lincoln," Sophie said into the phone after dialing the number of Angela Smith, a literary agent with whom she had worked in the past.

"Sophie? I don't believe it? Where have you been, honey?" Angela was glad to hear from her.

"I've been out of touch for a while. I was caring for my husband, who was very ill, but he died last spring. I've finally gotten myself busy writing again."

"I'm so sorry to hear about Carl. What are you writing? Am I going to be able to market this for you?" Angie was always the business woman.

"I'm having a lot of fun actually. I'm writing a story that has come to me from reading some old journals and diaries from when I was a kid. It will be an adventure story with some romance when I'm finished, and I'm probably about half of the way completed." Sophie was excited to be sharing her work with Angie again. She felt suddenly confident.

"Sounds interesting. But it's a bit of a diversion from your usual. How about sending me the first couple of chapters, and I'll take a look. There is a publisher who is looking for a similar genre, so this might just fit the bill. If they're interested, I'll see what I can do to get you an advance. We'll see if I can get the ball rolling on this."

"Thanks, Angie. I think you will like it. I'll get those chapters in the mail tomorrow, when I've had a chance to read through them again. Talk to you soon!"

Sophie was excited about the writing. She had completely immersed herself in the book, neglecting her assignment from her children to get her house in order. She placed the phone back in the cradle and walked out to the kitchen to make some tea. It was mid-afternoon, and she hadn't done a single thing around the house today. She reached up into the cupboard to retrieve a tea bag and a mug, along with some sugar, and waited for the water to boil.

"I wonder where Donnie is now", she thought to herself, tapping a pencil on the counter, where she had laid out a pad of paper to make a grocery list. It would be interesting to know what he thought of her writing. She had no idea where he might be living. Probably returned to Chicago, caught up in the fast life of the city. The phone interrupted her train of thought.

"Hello, Mom? It's Shirley. How are you today?"

"I'm just fixing a cup of tea. I've been writing all day, so I can't say I've accomplished much else." Sophie ran her fingers back through her hair. She wasn't about to apologize for how she spent her time to Shirley.

"What? You are spending all your time writing? What about the house and getting it ready to put on the market?" Shirley had a bossy tone in her voice that made Sophie at first feel a little guilty. Then she was irritated.

"Maybe I just don't really want to sell this house," Sophie replied, drumming the pencil with more intensity than before.

"But I thought this was all settled! We have all talked about you getting a place that's smaller and has less upkeep. Isn't that what we decided?" Shirley was raising her voice.

"Maybe that's what you have decided, but I just don't think I'm ready. I love my garden and working in the yard, and I have a lot of memories here. Cleaning out the attic has been good for me, but I want to spend time writing and enjoying my home. Thanks for making me talk about this, because I've decided at this very moment that I'm not putting the house up for sale. And that's my final word." Sophie's voice had escalated in response to Shirley.

"I don't believe this. Well, we'll talk about this later. I've obviously caught you at a bad time." Shirley's tone had turned to a sassy response.

Sophie couldn't believe her arrogance. "No, we will *not* talk about this later. I'm a perfectly capable and independent woman, and my decision is to stay in this house where I am happy. Shirley, you just need to understand that." She waited for Shirley's reaction.

After a short time, her tone much softer, Shirley responded. "Mom, you know we are all concerned about you being in that house all alone. It's just a worry for us to have you there. We thought you would be a lot happier in a smaller place with other people close around you. Maybe our thinking is wrong. I didn't mean to upset you."

"I know you have good intentions, but I'm very happy right where I am. I have good neighbors, good friends, and plenty to keep me busy. My writing absorbs a lot of my time, and you know how much I love it. So just don't worry about me."

"That's easier said than done. What are you writing about?"

"I'll tell you more about it later on. Angie Smith is going to take a look at it for me. I think it will be one of my best stories when it's finished. Thanks for asking,

Shirley." Sophie did not want to leave the conversation on a bad note.

"Well, it's good to see you writing again, and I will look forward to reading it. I'll talk to you later, Mom. Bye!"

Realizing that the kettle was whistling on the stove, Sophie poured the water over her tea bag and stirred it. Outside the leaves were still brilliant in the fall sun, and just beginning to fall from the very tops of the trees. A breeze blew in from the west, and Sophie remembered her Grandmother saying, "When the wind is from the west, the weather is at its best," or something to that effect. She smiled thinking of Grandma Palmer. There was always a quote or a saying for every occasion, some of them in German. She and Grandpa had lived on the farm before her folks, and she remembered the old car Grandpa drove back and forth from town to help out with the harvest and hay baling. Occasional visits to their house were a treat for her as well as for Dan.

She picked up the phone from the charger and pressed the speed dial #2. Dan should be home from work by now.

"Hi, Sis! What's up? Dan Palmer was always positive and had a penchant for his sister, especially after all these years.

"I just needed to talk to my big brother, I guess," Sophie responded. "I've decided to stay in the house here in Chatsworth for now. The kids have been pushing me to find a smaller place and get rid of some of the stuff in the house, but I've decided it's just not time yet. Do you think I'm just being stubborn?"

"You know what, Soph? You should do exactly what you want to do, and live your life the way you want. Are you concerned about staying there by yourself?" Sophie could hear Dan's concern in his voice, and she could picture the smile on his face as he spoke.

Sophie smiled to herself, noting that Dan was always the protective big brother. "No, I'm fine here. I told Shirley this afternoon that I have good neighbors and friends in the area. And I can do all the gardening and mowing myself yet at this point. It's my home."

"Then you are doing exactly the right thing. So what are you up to?"

Sophie could see his face––his brown eyes and dark hair with the smattering of silver. He had a broad smile and perfect teeth behind his greying beard and mustache.

"Oh, nothing much. Just doing some writing. I did get some junk out of the attic, and Tom hauled some stuff away for me. And I feel great. How about you?"

Sophie wasn't sure Dan would tell her if something was wrong.

"I'm great, as usual," he laughed. "I had the flu and a bad cold last week, but can't keep a tough old Illinois farm boy down for long! Things are pretty good at work, but there is talk of a buyout by a larger company. I've just decided to roll with the punches on that one. If I don't like what goes on with the new company, I can just retire and roam the countryside in our camper. Actually sounds pretty good to me!"

"Well, I'm glad you are doing okay. Keep me posted on the job situation."

Sophie and Dan talked about family and friends, but Sophie wasn't ready to share the subject of her book with him at this point. Dan still lived in Illinois, working in a small town not far from their home place. The farm had been sold when her parents died, and she and Dan had inherited the funds from the sale, giving each of them a nice nest egg. Dan had married Cathy Davenport, after dating her all through high school and college. Their three children were living all over the United States, and Dan and Cathy traveled a lot to see them and their grandchildren. Sophie and Dan had remained close, and he was a rock for her when Carl died, attending to details about the funeral and financial matters. She had learned quickly about managing her funds, and Dan had been more than willing to let her take the reins.

Sophie felt good about her decision to keep the house. She looked out at the garden and the lawn, then wandered briefly around the house, nodding her head that she had made the right decision, her decision, to stay right where she was. She fixed herself a bite of supper, tidied up the kitchen and returned to her office, where her story was waiting to be told.

Chapter 12
SOPHIE AND DONNIE

Sophie Writes

I turned the wheel on the tractor, trying to give the tires a wide enough berth to keep the trailer from dipping into the ditch. Donnie nodded his approval, but I noted that he was biting down on his lip as we rocked through the turn.

"Are you okay?" I asked, concerned about his leg.

"Just keep going, and don't worry about me, Sophie. When you get up close to the house, remember that when you stop, you have to push in both the pedals. If you put on the break without pushing in the clutch, you will kill the tractor, and we want to keep in running. Once you get it stopped, we will put the gear shift into neutral. You just pull back on the shifter until it moves freely from right to left. You can do it!" Donnie was coaching me for the next move.

"It looks like someone might be at home, Donnie. Maybe we can get some help."

I managed to get the tractor stopped, and pulled the gear shift back, as Donnie had instructed.

"You stay here, and I'll go see if someone is at home."

I climbed down off the tractor, urging Donnie to sit in the tractor seat until I got back. The walkway to the house was dark, but an outside light lit up the enclosed entry way to the house. I carefully opened the screen door and walked across the porch to knock on the door. It was slightly ajar.

I knocked once and listened, then knocked louder. "Anyone home?" I shouted. There was no answer. A small dog came to the door and scratched at it with her paw, pulling it open further.

"Hi, there, doggie," I said, stooping down to pet the dog, who was now on the porch with me. "Are you home by yourself?"

I peered through the open doorway to see if I could see anyone. It seemed odd that the door was not closed tightly, yet no one was at home. Calling out once again, I thought I heard a muffled noise from inside. Pushing the door open farther, I saw that someone was lying on the kitchen floor, and ran to the figure, not knowing what to expect. The man seemed to be out cold, and my heart was racing. Then another muffled sound came from behind me, and turning around, I was startled to see a woman tied up to a kitchen chair, her mouth taped with duct tape. She had a large bruise on her right cheek and was crying.

"What happened here?" I asked, trying to carefully remove the duct tape from the woman's mouth.

"Three men were here. One of them was our neighbor, Joe Dixon, and he was being held hostage by two other men. They hit my husband over the head with the butt of a gun and tied me up in this chair. We have to help my husband, Darrell!" She was out of her bindings and racing for the man on the floor.

"I'll get some water," I said, as I hurried to the kitchen sink and grabbed a dishtowel. I returned to the couple with the wet towel, and knelt alongside the woman, as she tried to revive her husband. Slowly, he began to come around, responding to the attention.

"Mary, are you okay?" Darrell asked, as he held his head and pushed himself up to a sitting position.

"I'm okay, thanks to this young lady," she said. "By the way, who are you, and why are you here?"

I looked at the two of them as though they were really just a part of a bad dream. "My friend and I were caught up in the storm. We finally got to Joe's place to get some help 'cause my friend has a broken leg.

Then these two guys caught Joe out in the barn, and Donnie and I hid under the bed so they didn't know we were there. When they left, we got on Joe's tractor and drove it here to find help. Donnie's really hurt bad, and we are so tired. We're afraid they are going to hurt Joe." I knew I was rambling, telling the story between sobs of fear and fatigue.

"Where's your friend now?" asked Mary.

"Donnie's out on the tractor, waiting for me. Our families are probably looking everywhere for us. Can you help us?"

Darrell stood up and grasped the back of the kitchen chair. He rubbed the top of his head, his fingers finding the bump and the cut the gun had left. He grabbed the dish towel from Mary and held it to the top of his head.

"The phones are down, so we can't call anyone to warn them about those guys and Joe. I'll get the car. We can get your friend in the car, and we'll see if we can get to town to the police to get some help for Joe. There's a clinic on the edge of town where we can take Donnie. Are you sure his leg is broken?" Darrell looked at me, taking in the sight of this poor girl, dirty from the water and tired from the day's ordeal.

"We think it is, for sure. Joe made a splint for it, but Donnie can't put any weight on it. He's in a lot of pain."

My composure was returning, just knowing that we would have some help.

Darrell ran out to get the car out of the garage. He helped Donnie down from his perch on the tractor and into the back seat, and Mary and I piled into the front seat of the car.

On our way into town, I described where my farm was located, and we determined that the two of us had been carried nearly five miles downstream by the flooding. Darrell and Mary knew my parents and Donnie's aunt and uncle. We all decided that the first order of business was to try to find someone to help Joe. He was in grave danger with those two men, as they were armed and unpredictable. I told Darrell that the two men had taken Joe so that he could get them some money in town. He had taken his checkbook, but had told them there wasn't much money in his account. Mary told Darrell that they had said pretty much the same when they left their house. They were going to town to get some more money.

At the edge of town, Darrell spotted the local Sheriff's car at a service station, and pulled in. The officer was on the phone quickly to alert other officers in the area about the situation with Joe. Then he told Darrell to take Donnie to the clinic and to get himself stitched up, and then to wait for the police there at the clinic.

Darrell drove the short distance to the clinic, where there was a doctor treating others who were injured by the storm or the flooding. A nurse took Donnie's name and helped him onto a table in a waiting room. Another nurse cleaned the cut on Darrell's head and sutured the wound. I was led into an area where I could clean up, and the nurse applied some antiseptic to the cuts on my arms and legs. The bruise on Mary's cheek had swollen, leaving her right eye nearly closed, but there was no permanent damage.

The doctor determined to move Donnie to the hospital in Lincoln, so that his leg could be X-rayed and set, and he was placed in an ambulance. I sat in the waiting room with Darrell and Mary to wait for the police to return. I leaned my head against Mary's arm and fell asleep.

Shouts from my mother awakened me. The police had contacted Dad and Mother, as well as Jack and Edna, to let them know that Donnie and I were safe.

"Oh, Sophie, are you okay?" Mother cried, as she gathered me into her arms. "We've been so worried about you!"

I immediately burst into tears. "I'm okay, but Donnie's got a broken leg." I continued to tell my parents all about our survival from the storm and all the events that followed. Just as I was finishing my story, the police car returned.

"Everything is under control, thanks to all of you. We found Joe's truck at the Speedy gas station, and set up to catch them on their way out of the store. We have both of them in custody, and Joe is fine. From what we have been told, this is a brave young lady." The police officer laid his hand on my shoulder. "At least we have one good outcome from this storm!"

I beamed at the attention and compliment, and blushed, my fair skin turning almost as red as my hair. But despite all the attention, I was concerned about Donnie.

"Daddy, will you take me to see Donnie?"

"Tomorrow, honey. Let's wait until tomorrow. I'm sure we could all use a good night's sleep tonight." Dad put his arm around my shoulders and pulled me close to him. "I'm not letting you out of my sight at the moment."

Chapter 13
DON

"Good morning, little Hope!" Don said, as the small animal curled up by his ear, her purring rousing him from a sound sleep. He couldn't believe he had actually brought home this kitten from the timber yesterday. Don threw back the covers and stretched his legs out onto the floor of the bedroom, reaching out with his toes for his slippers. He grabbed his robe from the poster on the bed and scooped up Hope to accompany him. On his way home from Illinois, he had stopped to pick up some cat litter and a box for the kitten, and had set the box up in the master bathroom of his condo. Hope scratched around in the box while Don headed for the kitchen to put on a pot of coffee. Hope followed him, running with her tail straight up in the air.

In the kitchen a small dish had been set up for food and water, still full from last night. Hope hungrily chewed on the tiny morsels. Don ground some fresh coffee for the well, filled the water reservoir, and clicked on the brewer. The refrigerator was rather bare, since he seldom cooked anything at home. "Maybe just a piece of toast would do me," he said, looking toward his new roommate, and took out some bread and peanut butter. He wasn't eager to take the time to go to the restaurant this morning, as he wanted to go over his painting from the previous day.

Feeling something tugging on his pant leg, he jumped aside to peer down at Hope, who had found his dangling pant leg irresistible. "Okay, let's be finding you something to play with." Don walked back to the bedroom and opened a drawer he hadn't looked into in some time. There were some balls of yarn in the drawer where Arlene had stored remainders of skeins. He selected one that was tightly wound, and tied the ends into the ball to keep it from unraveling, dragging it along with him back to the kitchen. Hope, who had followed him back to the bedroom, delighted in this new treat, and rolled around on the floor and swatted at it for the entire time it took Don to read the morning paper. Don found himself laughing at her, completely mesmerized by her antics. It felt so good to laugh.

Still in his pajamas and robe and slippers, Don took out his easel and his paints, and selected a new canvas to begin a painting of Hope. He sketched out lightly on the canvas the basic positions he wanted to capture of the kitten, and indicated the areas where her colors changed from white to black. With his pallet ready with the colors he wanted to use, he began to stroke out the essence of the enchanting creature before him. He was completely lost in his creation, realizing that he had never before painted an animated object.

While Don continued to paint, Hope had given up her play to curl up in the soft bed Don had purchased for her at the pet store. After consuming the entire pot of coffee and completing the basic structure of his painting, he realized that it was now eleven o'clock, and he hadn't even had a shower yet. He stood back and looked at the image before him, and smiled as his eyes strayed to Hope in her bed. "Not bad!"

Don cleaned his brushes and decided to go for a run. He donned a sweatshirt and jogging pants, then slipped into some tennis shoes, grabbed a stocking cap, and walked out into the brisk autumn air. As he started running at a slow jog, the aroma of fall was all around him. Somewhere some leaves were burning. The lawn care folks were mowing the grass, getting ready for the winter hibernation. Squirrels scurried to gather nuts, and chased each other up and down the tree trunks. Birds were already feeding at bird feeders set up by homeowners in the area, and the more ambitious were out with rakes to begin raking the leaves as they cascaded from the trees. The giant white ash trees had already begun to shed the brilliant yellow leaves, but the maples and oaks would retain their colors for a while longer.

The exercise was exhilarating, and Don returned to the condo feeling great. He quickly showered and decided to walk to the restaurant for some soup for lunch. Hope had decided to tackle his foot when he emerged from the shower, a game she would continue to play as they became more acquainted. Her claws were sharp, and it reminded Don that he would have to take her to the vet for her shots. He'd make that appointment this afternoon.

On his way to the restaurant, Don passed the usual stores along the way, and then came to the bookstore. Ben was working at the back of the store when he entered.

"What's up, Mr. Don?" he shouted to his most frequent customer.

"Just thought I'd stop in to look around and see what you have that's new in the store."

"I got in a new shipment today of the newest Harry Potter books, but you aren't reading these are you?"

"No, not my thing, actually. What else is new?"

Ben walked up toward the front of the store to see Don. "The newest novels are out in the front there," he gestured toward them. "But how about you? How's the painting coming along?"

Don smiled at his friend. "Just great, actually. I had my first class on Monday. Yesterday I took a trip to Illinois to find the farm where I used to visit when I was a kid, and I did some painting there. And brought home a kitten."

"Brought home a kitten? How did that happen?" Ben chuckled at the thought of Don with a kitten.

"She found me in the timber where I was painting. I couldn't find a mother cat, nor could I find anyone else who wanted her, so I've adopted Hope."

"Cute name. What color is she?"

Don gestured as he described Hope's size and then told his friend of the black and white colorings on her fur. He also related the morning antics and his attempt to capture her mischievousness in a painting.

"By the way, I heard today that Sophie Lincoln is coming out with a new novel. Her agent is already working on locations for book signings when it's published, probably in the spring. I think you like reading her books, don't you?"

"I do. It's a bit too much romance for me. But there's a Midwestern commonality about her writing that gets me really involved in her stories. Is there a hint about the story line?" Don was curious.

"Not yet. I'll let you know when I get the scoop on her book. They aren't expecting it to be published until probably March or April." Ben had a feather duster in his hand, and proceeded to dust off the shelves and book jackets as he talked to Don.

"I'll count on that. In the meantime, I have plenty to keep me busy. Catch you later!" Don was out the door and down the street in a few short steps. Ben smiled as he considered Don's apparent new outlook on life, demonstrated by his quick step and amiable expression.

Don ran into some of his cronies over lunch, and shared some laughs with them. Back at the condo, he checked on Hope's food dish, called the vet to set up an appointment to bring Hope in for a checkup, and fixed himself a cup of tea. Tomorrow night would be class night again, and his group would be working on entries to the contest. Putting his work out for public scrutiny was a little unnerving to Don, but he knew he was actually anticipating it as well.

"Okay, everyone. What have you come up with for a contest entry?" Chuck was ready to get them all entered in the contest and to help them with perfecting their projects. "Clay, how about you?"

"I spent some time out in my mom's flower garden, actually. I've started working on the colors of those asters and marigolds that are in bloom, and she has some statuary that I think will enhance the work." Clay had set up his canvas on the easel for all to view. Everyone applauded his work. Chuck made a few suggestions for Clay and addressed other students in the class who had started their paintings as well. Then he turned to Don. "Don, what about you?"

"Well, it's a long story, and actually a long drive. I went back to Illinois to a farm where I went as a boy, and found a good setting for a landscape." Don uncovered the painting he had kept hidden until this moment.

There was a gasp among the students, then applause for Don.

Chuck walked closer to the painting, taking in the colors and the buildings as Don had captured them. "My only suggestion is that you might want to show your viewers more of what is up closer to you. What do you see immediately around you that might be framing your view of this farm? See what you can do with that thought."

"I actually have another one to share with you." Don reached for his canvas of Hope and her yarn antics. Everyone came toward him, as he uncovered the picture.

"Don, you have done a great job with this!" exclaimed Clay. "Have you done anything like this before?"

"This is a first for me. Landscapes have always been appealing to me, but I found this kitten, and I so enjoyed her playing that I wanted to try to capture it."

Chuck studied the picture more closely. "Well, I'd say you have definitely accomplished your goal, Don. I think this is your contest entry. Actually, you might want to enter both of them." He put his hand on Don's shoulder. "Good job."

Don was soaring. The students and Chuck had all been very complimentary of his work. He set up his paints and thought about what was around him when he was painting the farm buildings and scenery around them. The old hut was there, and the thermos bottle he had found. It might be fun to have the old thermos in the picture. After several tries at giving the thermos just the right amount of space and color, he felt confident with his finished project.

Everyone chatted over their refreshments, talking excitedly about their subject matter and the feedback they might get from the contest. Entry forms were completed and entry fees were collected. The class was over much too soon in Don's estimation. He could have stayed among this group of individuals much longer. After class, he and Clay walked out together.

"How about a cup of coffee at Starbuck's?" Clay invited Don.

"Sure, it's not too late. As long as they have decaf!"

They walked to the Starbuck's, there in the same strip mall as the art store, after placing their materials in their cars.

"Don, you are really doing a great job with your painting," Clay started, after they had their coffee selections and had found a table.

"Why, thank you, Clay. You are also doing very well. Your style is much different from mine, as I tend to be pretty conservative. You have more of an abstract bent, and I admire that."

"Abstract. That's me. Are you married, widowed, divorced, or all of the above?" He smiled as he asked the question.

"Widowed. My wife died a few years ago, and I've really been in a funk for a while. It's really tough to lose a long-time partner. It's even harder to have to just stand by and watch them suffer."

Clay was quiet for a moment. "Sorry to hear that. I'm divorced but have recently found a lady who has brought me a lot of joy. I've even considered getting married again." He smiled. "Despite all that I've been through with the first wife."

"Do you have any kids?" Don knew that Clay was several years younger than he.

"Two, both boys. My ex and I shared custody of the kids after the divorce, but it's hard to be a dad when you aren't around them all the time. They are both out of high school now; one is working, and the other is in college. They're good boys." Clay beamed with pride describing the boys.

Don caught Clay's gaze. "My son had some real problems in college, so be sure to stay close to what they are doing. He's doing okay now, but that's after he suffered through some drug abuse and rehab. I also had a daughter, Annie, who died when she was 25. Marty and his family are really all I have left."

"Ever thought of getting back into the dating game?"

"No, not yet. I can't imagine myself with anyone besides Arlene."

"Well, I'll keep you in mind. Finding Callie was the best thing that has happened to me in a long time. She is really understanding about my obligation to my children, and she makes me laugh. That's worth a lot."

"Now don't go fixing me up with a blind date! I'm not ready for that." Don laughed. The two of them talked about some of their personal experiences and shared some of their work history as they finished their coffee. Don really enjoyed Clay. He seemed dedicated to his family, and he certainly shared a lot of common interests with Don. They parted ways as they walked back to their cars in the parking lot, decided to make the coffee stop after class each week, and invite others to join them.

Don was greeted at the front door of the condo by Hope, as she heard him turn his key in the lock. He picked her up and petted her, enjoying her chorus of purrs as she snuggled against his warmth.

"Imagine me with another woman," he said to Hope. "I think you are the only woman I need."

Don decided he would make another trip to Illinois this weekend. He might even make an overnight trip of it, and stop in to see some relatives in the Chicago area. But now he would also have to make arrangements for Hope, as she couldn't be traveling with him.

Don walked out of his apartment and knocked on the door across the hall. When Amelia opened the door he invited her over for a cup of tea, and then he introduced her to Hope. Amelia said she would be delighted to be able to help him out by caring for Hope and spending some time with her whenever he was gone. The two of them enjoyed watching Hope's antics as she pawed and jumped to catch a piece of string.

Chapter 14
SOPHIE

Sophie was lost in thought as she watched the leaves floating by her window, reflecting brilliant colors in the afternoon sun. She was trying to work on her story, but had run into a wall. The doorbell rang just in time to give her an escape from her funk.

She looked out the side window, then flung the door wide open. "Grace! So good to see you!" She greeted her good friend with a warm embrace.

"I was out running some errands, so thought I'd stop in to see you. You've been holed up in this house for weeks, and we have some catching up to do." Grace shed her coat and scarf, tossing them onto a chair in the living room as she led Sophie out to the kitchen. "It's such a beautiful day!"

Sophie poured glasses of iced tea and joined her friend at the table in the kitchen, where they could look out into the back yard.

"Your fall flowers are beautiful out there, Sophie. I wish I had your green thumb. How is the book coming along?"

"I'm just stuck at the moment, trying to get the story line to come together. It's kind of a tricky mix of reality and fiction. I have some ideas, but it's good you came by so I can walk away from it for a while. Tell me how things are going for you!"

Grace rolled her eyes, her face full of expression. "You know me, never a dull moment." She laughed at herself. Grace had a beautiful smile with perfect teeth. Her short blonde hair was highlighted and framed her round face, almost devoid of wrinkles. Blue eyes sparkled with her ever-positive outlook on life.

Sophie and Grace had been friends for many years. As couples, Grace and Fred Walters had traveled with Sophie and Carl, and they had enjoyed many a riotous card game at this kitchen table. The two of them had been great support for Sophie while Carl was ill and after his death, taking her places and making her feel a part of the social scene as a single woman. She was very grateful for their friendship, especially Grace's.

Grace continued. "I stopped by the college today in Staley and found out there's an art exhibit and contest there next Friday and Saturday, and I thought you might want to go with me. Some of the work will be for sale, and it might be fun to see what the students are creating. The competition is open to any amateur artist, so who knows. There might be some budding artist there at an inexpensive price. What do you say?"

"Sounds like fun. Saturday would probably be best for me. Let's go later in the morning, and we can go to lunch while we are there. Is Fred going along?"

"No, let's leave him home. This will be a girls' day out!" Grace reached across the table and patted Sophie's arm.

They talked about children and grandchildren, and all that had been going on in their lives. Sophie shared her frustration with her daughters, feeling they were pushing her to leave her home. Working on the book was giving her some outlet, and she related to Grace how she had sort of put Shirley in her place last week.

"I'm not exactly pushing up daisies yet!" Sophie laughed.

"I guess not! This is such a great house, Sophie, and you should stay here as long as you like. Fred read me a paragraph out of an article the other day about how a person who has experienced the death of a spouse should wait to make any major decisions for at least two years. And Carl has only been gone for six months. You have plenty of time." Grace walked to the patio doors to have a better look out into the back yard.

"When I was cleaning out the attic, I ran across some things that I am using in my new book, Grace." Sophie took the woven ring and the chain from an envelope in a drawer in the kitchen. "These were given to me by a boy who was visiting his aunt and uncle on a farm across the timber from ours when we were kids. It's been so much fun reminiscing about that summer."

"Where is this boy now? Do you know?" Grace was curious about her friend's treasures.

"I have no idea. He lived in Chicago at the time, and I never saw him after that summer when I was about eleven. I found some old journals I had kept at the time, and that's the basis for my book. His aunt and uncle are gone from the farm, and he went to school somewhere here in Iowa, but I suspect he has moved back to the city. It would be really hard to try to run him down, but it would be fun to see what he remembers." Sophie smiled at the thought.

"Who knows? You just might cross paths again someday. In any case, I've got to get on with my errands. I'll pick you up next Saturday at about nine if that's okay with you."

Sophie helped Grace with her coat and walked her to the front door.

"See you then."

Back in the office, Sophie read through the last chapter she had completed to see if she could jump start her writing.

Chapter 15

SOPHIE CONTINUES HER STORY

I remember that Jack called Dad to let him know that they were bringing Donnie back to their house the following day, and that he was in a cast from the knee down. The doctor had said that the splints had helped to hold the break in place so that it wasn't compounded, and that the break was clean. But Donnie had instructions to keep the leg elevated for a couple of days. He was to stay in bed with it propped up on pillows. Jack said I was welcome to come to see him at any time. Donnie's parents were traveling, so wouldn't be able to get him for another week. Jack was sure he would enjoy the company.

June 16, 1954 – Dad took me over to the Ribold's house today, after we heard from Mr. Ribold that Donnie had been brought back to their house from the hospital. Donnie's parents are on a trip to Europe, so he can't go home until they return. I felt so sorry for him, when I saw him in the bed with his leg in a cast and propped up on a pillow. He said it didn't hurt much anymore, and he had some pills for the pain. We set up a checkerboard on a table by his bed and played checkers for a while. I told him about a book I was reading, and he wants me to bring it and read to him tomorrow. His aunt is getting him some paints and brushes so he can do some painting to pass the time. Mom says I can only stay for a couple of hours each day, as I have chores to do at home. Boring!

Over the next several days, Donnie and I enjoyed playing cards, Monopoly, and checkers, and I read to him from my book. The book was an adventure story, so Donnie was interested in the outcome of the characters.

June 20, 1954 – Donnie's parents called today when I was at Jack and Edna's to tell them they had arrived at home and would be down to pick him up tomorrow. It's so sad to think I won't see him again for a while. I think I'll write him a poem.

Good friends are very special
When you are just a kid.

They make your life exciting
Thinking of all the things you did.

Donnie is a special friend,
And I won't soon forget
The fun we've had together
As though we were one matched set.

He's going to Chicago now
To see his mom and dad.
I hope he won't forget me,
As I'll be really mad.

I think I'll give him this poem tomorrow, and it will
make him laugh.

I did give Donnie the poem. And to my surprise, he presented me with a small box that contained two items. One was a ring woven of twine that he had made in Boy Scouts the year before. The other was a silver chain. I knew I had seen him wearing it.

"Sophie, I love the poem, and I won't forget you. I wouldn't want you to be mad at me. Maybe I can come back next summer, and we'll spend some more time together. My leg will be healed and we can go bike riding." Donnie seemed sincere.

"That would be great, Donnie. I'll keep these forever and think of you. Thank you." I reached for his hand.

Donnie held my hand tightly, drawing back quickly when his mom came into the room.

"You must be Sophie. I want to thank you for taking care of our Donnie during the storm," Donnie's mom said. "Donnie, we have to get going to get back to Chicago. Sophie, we'll be seeing you."

Donnie stood up with his crutches and swung himself expertly out to the car. "Good-bye, Sophie!" he called, as his dad closed the door after him. The last I saw of him was as he looked out the window of the car to wave good-bye.

July 5th – I got a short letter from Donnie today. He gets his cast off in a week, if the break is healed. I've written several letters, but this is the first one I've gotten. We all went to the fireworks in town last night, and I walked around the festival grounds with my friends.

As the summer continued on into August, and after school started in September, I didn't get any more letters from Donnie. I was busy with school and my chores at home. I saw Donnie's Aunt Edna at the grocery store, and she told me that Donnie had made the basketball team at his school. She and Jack were planning to go to Chicago for the Thanksgiving holiday, and hoped to be there when Donnie was playing. As an eighth grader, Donnie was going to be starting for the team. I told her to tell him hello for me, feeling very sad.

Chapter 16
SOPHIE

Sophie saved the program on her computer, and shut it down for the evening. She knew she wanted to work on the eventual outcome of the story, but didn't want to start on it late in the afternoon. She would work on it again later. It would take some time to plot out their reunion. She decided she needed to do some research in the meantime.

Feeling elated with her progress for the day and her thoughts on the book, Sophie went back up into the attic to work on her cleaning job, finally getting through the items in the trunk and setting up piles of clothes and papers for Tom. She ran across an aerial photo of the old farm homestead and reminisced about the various buildings. In addition to the old farm house, there was an old granary, the old machine shed, and the new corncrib she remembered her dad and the neighbors building. The old chicken house was there as well as the brooder house. Three poplar trees faced the road, while the apple and cherry trees lined the driveway. The windmill stood proudly beside the barn.

"Wouldn't it be interesting to drive back to Illinois to see the farmstead and visit my folks' grave sites?" Sophie pondered the idea. She was certainly capable of making the trip alone, and she was excited about the idea. She would call Tom to let him know where she was, and make the trip tomorrow. If she got up early, she could easily drive there and back in one day, or maybe even spend the night on Saturday and drive back on Sunday.

Tom was a little apprehensive about the idea of Sophie making the trip by herself, but agreed to keep it to himself not share with Shirley and Trudy. Sophie agreed to call him on Saturday to let him know she had arrived safely. He also wanted to know if she were going to spend the night and where.

With her plans in place and Tom on her side, Sophie packed up a small overnight bag and some snacks, filled her car with gas, and turned in early to get a good night's rest. She rented a book on tape from the library, so she could listen to it on her drive. Tomorrow would be an interesting day, she was quite sure.

The trip to Illinois seemed to go quickly with the reader on the tape keeping Sophie's mind absorbed in the story. The hours virtually flew by. She almost missed her exit onto I-74, caught up in the heart-stopping intrigue of *Intensity*. With just a couple of stops along the way, Sophie arrived in Clarion around noon and stopped at the café where she and her family had eaten so many meals. As she entered the cafe, she noted that basically the interior hadn't changed much over the years. The old wallpaper had been removed and the assortment of antique tools and ad posters appeared more prominent against the solid color of the walls. The stools by the counter had been recovered and the window treatments had been updated. She walked toward a booth along the windows and took off her coat.

"What can I get for you?"

Sophie turned to see a man in his fifties, wearing a white apron over his jeans and a flannel shirt. She studied his eyes and face for a moment.

"Jeff? Jeff Largent, is that you?" Sophie asked, excited to see an old friend of the family.

"Yes, I'm Jeff. But I'm afraid I don't know you." He was studying Sophie's face, searching for a name.

Sophie smiled. "I'm Sophie Palmer, well, Sophie Lincoln now. Did you take over this place from your folks?"

"Well, I'll be. Sophie Palmer. I haven't seen you for years!" He shook her hand with enthusiasm. "My wife and I run the place now, and we are really busy here. My wife loves reading your books. I'm sure she has several, but I haven't seen a new one in a while. What brings you to Clarion?"

"I just decided to take a drive today. I live in Iowa, and it's only about four hours' drive. I wanted to visit the old farm place and the folks' graves in the cemetery. The fall weather has been so beautiful, and it's been fun driving and just getting out."

"Well, good to see you, and welcome back to town. Can I get you something for lunch? The specials are on the board."

Sophie gave him an order for the vegetable soup of the day and a salad, along with a cup of coffee. She looked out the window into the town square for familiar sites, feeling a sense of belonging. Cars drove around the square as they had done so many years before, and people strolled around the courthouse in the center of the block. The buildings looked bright and colorful, apparently having a face lift since she had last seen them. Jeff returned with her lunch.

"Mind if I sit with you a minute? I'd love to catch up on where you've been and what you've been up to."

Jeff and Sophie talked as she ate her soup and salad, as Jeff told her about his parents, his kids, and his grandkids. Sophie gave him a thumbnail sketch of her own life as well.

"Say, Jeff, do you know what happened to the Ribold family? Are there any of them around here anymore?"

"Jack and Edna had a son and a daughter. The daughter lived in Chicago, but the son, Alex, was a dentist here in town for a long time. I think Alex lives out at the Manor at the edge of town. His kids grew up and left the area. I'd guess he's somewhere in his eighties. Pretty spry old guy, though. Sharp as a tack!"

"Do you ever, by any chance, see anything of Jack's nephew, Donnie? I only knew him as a kid, but wondered about him."

"Actually, Don stopped by here a while back. I hadn't seen him in years, and barely recognized him. He said something about doing some landscape painting in the area. He's had a pretty sad life. His wife died of cancer, and he lost a daughter when she was pretty young. He has one son, Marty, and lives somewhere in Iowa."

"Really? Well, that's a coincidence, isn't it? But it's a big state."

"Sorry I don't know any more than that. I do have to work while I'm here, you know."

"Well, listen, this has been fun. But I need to get moving. I want to stop out at the farm and don't want to be too late getting back onto the road back to Iowa. The lunch was great, as was the company." Sophie smiled and laid out enough cash to cover her meal and a tip. "I'll stop by again sometime."

She left the restaurant and drove by the Manor on the way out of town. "What are the odds that the old dentist would know where Donnie had gone?" she wondered aloud, quickly passing the thought as she turned onto the blacktop road to the old farm.

She turned into the driveway of the farmstead and stopped the car to take in the buildings and the house. Some of the old, smaller buildings had been torn down, and a new machine shed stood out prominently behind the house. The house had newer siding, but was still white. It appeared that a porch and a sun room had been added, making the house seem larger than she remembered it. The back porch had also been enclosed. Sophie pulled her car on up into the driveway, stopping in front of the hedge where a new concrete approach had been poured. Opening the car door, she could smell the unmistakable aroma of freshly mowed hay. She walked up to the back door and knocked.

There was no answer. She wondered who lived here on the farm now.

Surely no one would mind if she walked back across the field to the timber. She pulled her car up beside the old barn, locked the doors, and started off across the field. The fall plowing had been completed, making it a difficult for Sophie to walk across the clods of dirt. Within a few moments, she had arrived at the timber. Making her way through the undergrowth, watching for poison ivy and thistles, she found the old hideout, now pretty much in shambles.

A flood of memories came back to her at the sight of the old logs, bales, and boards. As she looked around, she noted that the area around the hut had been trodden down, as though someone had been there. She saw an old Thermos bottle lying among the grasses and stooped to pick it up. "Can this be the one I brought out here to meet Donnie that day?" she asked herself.

Carrying the thermos, Sophie walked far enough to be able to look down into the creek from the bank, and then to look across at the Ribold place. It too had changed some from what she remembered. She turned to walk back across the field, looking back only for a moment, feeling as though she had heard the ghosts of children behind her.

The farmstead was still deserted when Sophie returned. She put the Thermos bottle in the back seat of the car and headed back toward Clarion. As she approached the edge of town, she decided to stop by the Manor to see if Donnie's cousin, the dentist, might know of his whereabouts.

"I'm looking for Alex Ribold," said Sophie when she walked up to the information desk.

"Mr. Ribold isn't here this afternoon," the nurse replied. He has gone out with another gentleman who stopped by to pick him up. Can I give him a message for you?"

"Oh, no. He doesn't really know me. But thanks, anyway."

Sophie walked back to her car and drove to the other side of town, stopping at the grocery store to pick up a cemetery wreath to take to where her parents were interred. The old cemetery was on the top of a hill just outside of town. The wind blew relentlessly, no matter what time of year, and was very cold in the late autumn afternoon. She smiled as she looked at the headstones, and remembered how her mother used to bring her here to walk among the gravestones. She had talked about how many of those buried so long ago were related. Sophie placed the wreath in front of the headstones and got into her car to begin her drive back to Iowa. The narrator of *Intensity* came on as she turned the key, "Chapter 15."

Sophie was quickly rapt with the continuing story on the tape. Only brief moments of thought distracted her as she thought back to her childhood, then thought ahead to completing her manuscript for publishing. Having seen the farm and after her talk with Jeff Largent, she began to develop the story in her mind.

Chapter 17
SOPHIE AND GRACE

The exhibit hall at the college in Staley was busy with people anxious to view the art work on display. The prizes had been awarded and ribbons of many colors were displayed on the winning entries. Sophie and Grace had gotten a late start and had stopped for a cup of coffee, so they were a little late in arriving.

"Okay, so you are looking for flowers, and I'm looking for whatever, is that right?" Grace teased Sophie.

"Well, not necessarily. I might find something else I really enjoy. I'm not sure I'm in the mood for buying anything, but I do want to look."

They started off following the crowd to the right as they entered the exhibits area. Sophie was immediately drawn to a tiny sculpture of wild flowers, done with copper pieces and displayed with a photograph of the flower. She thought it was fascinating how the artist had completely duplicated the flower in shape and color, and stopped to try to catch the artist's attention.

"I'm going on ahead, and you can catch up." Grace wasn't interested in all the details of the work.

Sophie talked with the artist about his methods and how he had become interested in the work. The young man was a student of sculpture at the college and had been encouraged by his professor to pursue this medium. He told Sophie about his subjects and the research on each item. Books on wild flowers had given him the details of the flowers in his work. Each of the petals had been crafter from bits of copper, as were the leaves, and then painted the color of the flowers in the pictures he had found. The intricacy of the work was what captured Sophie's attention.

Meanwhile, Grace had found a landscape that had taken a first place ribbon. The artist was not in the area, and she couldn't read his signature, but it didn't really matter that much to her. She agreed to the price that had been placed on the item, paid the individual attending the booth, and had it wrapped. By the time Sophie caught up with Grace, the canvas had already been concealed in the wrapping.

"What did you find already?" asked Sophie.

"I don't want you to see it until I get it framed and hanging on my wall. I think you'll like it, because it looks like a farm in Iowa or Illinois."

Sophie rolled her eyes and smiled. "You are too much. I'll bet you don't even know the artist's name."

"No, I can't read it, but I don't care. I just like the painting."

They walked on around the room to view other displays. At the front of the room, a photograph had been placed on an easel, with a note that the grand prize acrylic exhibit had been sold. In the photograph was a picture of the canvas that had sold; a small black and white kitten playing with a ball of yarn. The two of them smiled at the artist's capture of the personality of the kitten and shared an "awwwww!"

Chapter 18

HOLIDAY TIMES

"You sold my landscape, too?" asked Don, as he came back to the area where his painting had been displayed.

"I did. The Art Department will issue you a check for your paintings, less the commission they are charging for the show." Chuck was excited for Don for the sale of the two paintings. "You are really on a roll, Don!"

"It's kind of hard to part with those. Do you know who bought the landscape?"

Chuck looked around the arena. "I don't see the lady anymore. She really liked it, and she said she had the perfect place to display it." He patted Don on the shoulder. "You'll just have to get busy and get more completed."

The holiday season was a busy time. Don made a couple of more trips to Illinois to capture the late fall and winter scenes, and included the snowfalls in his paintings. He had even stopped at the Nursing Home Manor to take his cousin Alex for a drive. He created more paintings of Hope, as she continued to amuse him with her antics. She had found a spot on the extra pillow on the bed, and had slept there with Don every night. When he had to be away, his neighbor was always ready to care for her. Playthings for her included a climbing tower covered in carpeting, an old sock tied in a knot, and a rubber ball with a tin ball inside.

Don had started to paint some of the more historic areas of Staley, including the old mill, various aspects of the public park area, the older buildings downtown, and views of the lake covered in a blanket of snow. He and his fellow students continued to enjoy their time together at Chuck's. His advice and guidance were always beneficial.

Don had met Clay's girlfriend, Callie, and had been invited to dinner with them on occasion. Callie had prepared a big Thanksgiving feast and had invited Don to join them. Marty and Janet were with her parents, so he was free. He found their relationship very refreshing, and Clay seemed to be very happy. The two art students had continued to go out after class, and were now accompanied by the rest of the group most of the time. The network of support had been good for all of them. Clay had really improved his painting, but was limited on time to spend with his art because of his work schedule.

Clay and Don agreed to do some Christmas shopping together one Saturday, so Don drove the two of them to Chicago. Clay had never been to the city, so Don thought it would be fun to show him around. They took in the Aquarium, The Water Tower, the Brookfield Zoo, and other sites around the city. Clay was in awe of Lake Michigan, the buildings, and the people.

"This is a magnificent place, Don!" Clay announced. "Don't you sometimes wish you were still here in the city?"

"No, not really. I enjoy the smaller towns, and I can always go back to Chicago. Let's go out to Oakbrook and do a little shopping there."

Don drove to the mall, where he and Clay wandered around for hours looking for ideas for family members. Don found the boys each a Chicago Bears sweatshirt and cap and bought Marty a new driver for his clubs. Marty had given him a hint on a perfume for Janet, and he found that as well. He assisted Clay in locating his gift list items, and the two of them collapsed into a booth at a coffee shop for a break before heading back to Staley.

"So, are you getting something special for Callie for this Christmas?" Don asked, smiling wryly at Clay.

"I thought about it. I think if I asked her to marry me, she would say 'yes'." Clay was grinning like a schoolboy.

"Are you ready for the commitment?"

"I think so. I couldn't do any better for myself than Callie, in my estimation. She is good to me and to my kids, and they really like her. It's just taking that step, you know?"

"Well, no, actually I don't know. It's pretty hard for me to imagine being in your shoes after all these years. Who would want an old fart like me?"

"We'll see, Don Ribold. One of these days, the tables will be turned, and you'll be looking for advice from me on how to ask some pretty lady to marry you."

They laughed and enjoyed their coffee before starting the journey home to Iowa. Don cherished their friendship and their mutual love of the arts.

"Okay, class, the holidays are over, and it's time to get back to work. How many of you have some works you could put on display, if we were to have an exhibition here at the store?" Chuck addressed Don's class at the first meeting after Christmas.

Several of the class members responded positively, curious as to Chuck's interest in setting up the exhibit.

"Then we'll plan to have an exhibit here in late March. That will give you some time to put together some of your work, get some things framed, and decide on a price."

"Can you help us with that part of it? That's my biggest challenge: What to charge for my paintings?" Don spoke for the whole group.

"Once we get some items here, and decide how we are going to lay all this out, we can talk more about price. For tonight, let's get a start on the still life I have brought for this evening's class." Chuck directed their attention to the new arrangement on the velvet backdrop. The arrangement looked like a table once positioned beside a sofa. There was a pipe, a small vase of flowers, an ashtray, and a half eaten apple. Interesting combinations for sure.

The next morning, Don walked in the cold January air to the restaurant for breakfast, stopping by the bookstore on his way back to the condo.

"How's Michelangelo getting along?" Ben teased, as Don came into the store.

"Very funny, Ben. I'll have you know I'm going to have some of my work displayed at Chuck's in an exhibit he is setting up, sometime in March. How about that?"

"Good for you! Do you want to have some things on display here in the store?"

"Would you do that for me? I have some that are winter scenes that people might like, and you could certainly have a commission on the ones that sell."

"Sure. Just bring some things by. It would probably be best if they are framed, as they will sell better that way." Ben seemed truly interested in displaying some of Don's work.

"I have to do that anyway for the exhibit at Chuck's. There's a frame shop out in the shopping center, so I need to get on that right away. I'll get back to you when I get some things together. Thanks, Ben. I appreciate it."

"No problem. This is a business arrangement." Ben winked at him.

Don wandered around the store looking for book titles that interested him, and selected a new mystery, paid for his selection, and went on about his walk back to the condo.

The holidays for Sophie were lonely and long. The kids and their families were all there for Thanksgiving, Shirley pitching in to help with the cooking and cleanup. Christmas was at Trudy's, her home decorated to the hilt with all the seasonal trappings. Her home was filled with the aroma of bayberry and pine, with candles burning in each room of the house. The atmosphere was festive, but the entire season was somewhat depressing for Sophie. She bought gift cards for everyone, not really in the mood for shopping for individual presents. It just wasn't the same without Carl. Shirley had invited her to go shopping with her, but she had turned her down, using her manuscript as an excuse.

Sophie's latest book was completed by the end of the first week of January. She had submitted it for editing to her agent, who was excited about the story line and characters. Having the book completed was also a letdown for Sophie. She had managed to get lost in the story and her journals as an escape from reality. Nothing had come to her as a subject for a new book as yet, so she felt as though she was in limbo. Angie would be setting up book signings for her, so that would get her out and about. Being with people and having appointments were helpful in keeping her going. The kids had backed away from pushing her to get rid of the house, so she wasn't under pressure from them anymore.

Chapter 19
SOPHIE'S STORY CONTINUES

"Sophie, you have to come over to see the painting! I have it framed and hung in the living room." Grace called early one Friday morning in March.

"Good grief, Grace. I forgot all about that painting. Did you ever figure out who the artist is?"

"No, but I'm going to Staley to an exhibit this weekend, so maybe I'll find out then. Want to go with me?"

"I can't. I have to fly to New York to sign the contracts and meet with Angie about the book. We're going to go over my schedule for book signings then. I'm excited about it."

"You should be. I'm excited for you! Can you come over for coffee?"

"Give me time to get my shower and dress, and I'll walk over. It looks like it's a beautiful spring day."

I grabbed my purse and jacket on my way out the door to walk the short distance to Grace's home. A light breeze made my eyes water, but it carried the scents of new blooms. Buds were appearing on the trees, and it occurred to me that they might be frozen with a late frost. I reached Grace's front door in quick time and rang the doorbell.

Grace opened the door wide for me to enter. Then she took me by the arm to lead me into the living room. "There it is!"

I was taking my jacket off, but stopped with it just off my shoulders, staring at the painting before me. I gasped, "Grace, it's my home in Illinois!"

"What? You must be kidding. You mean your farm back in Illinois? How can that be?"

"I don't know. Someone has painted this from the timber looking out toward the farm. I was just there a few months ago, so I know that is the place."

"You were there? Right there where the artist was when it was painted?"

"Yes, and I could see then that someone had been there. And you still don't know the name of the artist, right?"

"No, I don't. Can your read it?"

I leaned into the painting, trying to make out the signature, but to no avail. The artist had evidently decided to use some kind of stroke to identify him or herself. "Well, I have to know who this is. You say you are going back to Staley this weekend?"

"Yes, there's an exhibit at an art studio there in the shopping center. The owner is displaying all the works of his students, and they'll be for sale. I'll look for the signature on another painting, and see what I can find out. I don't know if the same artist will appear at this show, but I promise I'll try to find out. This is really amazing. I have your farm on display in my living room! How weird is that?"

"Will you sell it to me, Grace?" I begged, knowing my friend was really fond of the painting.

"Sophie, I love you, but I'm not sure about that. I'll have to think on it. Let's go have a cup of coffee and a muffin."

I glanced at the painting for one more look, as Grace escorted me out to the kitchen. I could hardly believe my eyes.

For the next several weeks I was caught up in a whirlwind of activity, making trips to New York to promote the book, as well as Atlanta, San Francisco, Los Angeles, Minneapolis, and Miami for book signings. Thankfully, an early spring had made the traveling easy, with no snow delays in Iowa to hamper my flights. Angie had set up the introductions in each location. The local bookstore chains had offered me time slots for lectures and presentations on the book and my experiences as a writer. I enjoyed the notoriety and found myself completely absorbed in the adventure. The readers were bringing in books for signatures, and were very complimentary about the characters and the story.

I was settled into my new life as a widow and an author. The extra money from the book contract had given me a chance to do some work on the house to update the flooring and drapes, and Tom had helped me out with some painting to give some of the rooms a facelift. I barely had time to work in the garden, leaving me frustrated with its ragged appearance. The perennials were coming up, but I hadn't had any time to begin to shop for annuals to plant in some of the containers. Maybe this weekend, I would have a chance.

The airport was noisy with Sunday travelers milling about with their carry-on luggage, waiting for flights or shuttles to various terminals in Chicago, where I was catching a connecting flight to the Chatsworth Regional Airport. As I walked through the hallways to the G terminal, I spied a coffee shop and decided to stop for a cup of coffee. I realized that I hadn't eaten anything since morning, and my stomach felt queasy. The attendant took my order for a cinnamon scone to accompany the coffee, and I settled at a table near the rail around the seating area.

It felt good to just sit for moment. Getting around in the cities was a challenge for me, even though Angie had supplied me with good information on getting cabs and buses to get to my destinations. The concierge at the hotel had also been very accommodating.

I glanced at my watch. It was another hour before the flight, so I would have plenty of time with just a five-minute walk left to the gate. I reached down into my bag and pulled out the *People* magazine, laying it out on the table. I smiled at a distinguished man who walking toward me, then took a seat at a table behind me.

"Are you Sophie Lincoln?" A young woman approached me and handed me my book, the picture displayed on the back cover.

"Why, yes, I am." I smiled and blushed at the recognition.

"Could I have your autograph in my copy of the book? I hate to interrupt you."

I took the book and opened the front cover. "What is your name?"

"Martha. Or M.J. would be fine," she responded, seemingly excited about getting her book personally signed by the author.

"There you are Martha. Have you enjoyed the book?"

"Yes, I have. I grew up on a farm, so I can really relate to the story."

I handed her the book. "I'm so glad you enjoyed it." Martha took the book and left, walking quickly down the terminal hallways to her flight. I watched her, always amazed at a perfect stranger recognizing me in unusual places. I shook my head and looked down at the magazine.

"Sophie Lincoln?" It was another voice, this time from behind me. I turned to see the man who had walked toward me earlier. "I understand you are coming to Staley, Iowa, for a book signing. I go the book store quite frequently, and we are all anxious to hear your presentation."

"Yes, I believe that is in May. I think I'll probably be exhausted by the time I get to Staley. It's been quite a spring for me. Have you read the book?"

"No, not yet. I'm usually drawn to adventure stories rather than love stories, and I understand your book is a love story?"

"Well, yes, it is. But it's a bit of an adventure as well, and I think it speaks to many people our age. If you get a chance to read it before I get to Staley, I'll be looking forward to your comments. And what do you do for a living?" I had always enjoyed learning about the interests and careers of people travelling.

"Recently, I have enjoyed painting. I don't have any of my work with me, or I'd share it with you. I retired some time back, but painting has given me a breath of fresh air, so to speak. Listen, I have to get to my plane, but I'll look forward to seeing you again in Staley. And I'll be sure to pick up the book!" He picked up his briefcase and his jacket and hurried away to reach his gate.

"What a delightful man," I said aloud, watching him as he walked away. It dawned on me that I didn't know his name. He had grey sprinkled into his dark hair, giving him a suave appearance, and he was in excellent shape. His lanky frame was emphasized by the cuffed pants and bold blue shirt.

I caught the plane back to Chatsworth, where Grace was waiting for me as I emerged from the baggage area. I tossed my bags into the back seat of Grace's car and collapsed into the front seat.

"You look exhausted!" said Grace, sizing up my expression. "I'll bet you could use a glass of wine and a home cooked meal."

"That sounds wonderful. I had a continental breakfast this morning, then a scone at the airport in Chicago, so I haven't really had anything healthy all day. Are you offering?" I laughed at Grace, appreciative of her friendship and concern.

"Yes, I am. I have a roast in the oven, and a bottle of Riesling chilling in the fridge. We'll have you perked up in no time."

"Either that, or I'll be asleep on the couch!" I was so glad to be home. The two of us caught up on the events of the weekend. I told her all about my trip to Miami, the hotel where I stayed, and the places that had been set up for my book signings. We pulled into Grace's garage, leaving the bags in the car, and joined Fred in the kitchen.

"Take a look at this, Sophie," said Fred, handing me a painting. "Isn't this the cutest picture?"

I took the painting from him and admired the kitten portrayed there, batting at a bell suspended from a ribbon.

"How delightful!" I exclaimed. Then I noticed the signature on the painting. It was the same illegible scrawl as on the painting in the living room.

"Did you find out the name of the artist?" I turned to look at Grace.

"Yes I did, actually. His name is Don Ribold. He is an art student at the studio where the paintings were displayed." Grace was stirring the gravy on the stove, so she didn't see my face turn ashen.

"Did you say Don Ribold?" I was in shock. It had to be the same Don Ribold I had known so many years ago. "Did you meet him?"

"What's wrong with you? You look like you have seen a ghost!" Grace grabbed my arm, looking into my eyes.

"Grace, Don Ribold is the boy from my journal who disappeared from my life so many years ago." I sat down heavily on a kitchen stool.

"Of course! I should have known the name. I just didn't make the connection!"

"Did you meet him? Do you know where he lives?"

"Grace looked at Fred, then back at me. "I guess he lives in Staley. I think there is a picture of him on a flyer they were handing out at the exhibit." Grace walked over to her purse, and took out some papers she had placed inside. "Yes, here is the picture of him," She handed me the flyer.

I looked at the picture in stunned disbelief. Then I put my hand over my eyes, unable to believe the series of events taking place.

"I was talking to this very man today at the airport in Chicago. Someone asked me for my autograph, and he heard my name. He knew I was going to be in Staley for a book signing and mentioned it to me. We were just making small talk, and he never introduced himself. This is too unbelievable. Can I keep this, Grace?"

"Sure, you can have it. Are you going to try to get in touch with him?"

"I have to. Grace, you won't believe what a nice man he is. And it would be so much fun to catch up with each other after all these years." I could hardly contain my excitement, my fatigue from my travels now forgotten.

The three of us ate the supper Grace and Fred had prepared. Grace took me home, teasing me about calling Don.

"Now you watch out for that handsome gentleman in the picture. He might be dangerous for you!" We laughed and made jokes about me pursuing a relationship with him.

"Remind him that he has already given you a ring!" Grace teased, as she pulled into my driveway.

"Oh, stop it, Grace. He might even be married for all I know, and I'm not exactly looking for a man, you know."

"Can you get those bags okay?" Grace put the car in park to release the locks.

"I've got them, Grace. And thanks for supper!"

I made my way to the door to unlock it, and waved to Grace as I entered the house, pulling the suitcase behind me. I closed the door and locked it, moving on through the house to put the suitcases in the bedroom, and turning lights on along the way.

The house felt a little chilly since I had turned the thermostat down before I left, so I grabbed a sweater from the closet. The furnace responded as the dial returned to its normal setting, immediately sending warm air to the registers.

I looked through the mail the postal carrier had inserted into the mail slot, pitching the junk mail into the waste basket, and placing the bills in the basket on the counter in the kitchen. Tom had left a note to say he had changed the filter in the furnace and added salt to the water softener on Saturday, and hoped I had a good trip to Florida. Tom's notes always made me smile. I put on a teakettle of water and removed a tea bag from the box.

Noticing my purse on the counter where I had dropped it, I pulled the brochure from the pocket. The picture was very clear. The eyes, the smile—they were still the same as on the boy I remembered. There was a natural wave in his hair, now slightly grey. I ran my fingers over the features of his face. Could I do it? Could I call him?

The whistle on the teakettle distracted me for a moment, as I poured the water and added a little sugar to the tea. Taking the portable phone in my hand, I dialed the number on the brochure. One ring. Two rings. Three rings, then . . .

"Hello?" A man's voice on the other end of the phone.

"Hello?" He repeated his question, as the words were caught in my throat. Just before he could hang up the phone, I responded.

"Is this Don Ribold?"

"Yes, it is. May I ask who is calling?"

"It's Sophie Lincoln."

"Sophie Lincoln? We just met today at the airport. How did you find me and get my number? I remembered that I hadn't even introduced myself."

"It's a long story, Don. Do you have a moment?"

"Sure. I'm all ears."

"What would you say if I told you my name is Sophie Palmer Lincoln?"

There was a silence on the other end of the phone line.

"Sophie Palmer? The Sophie Palmer I knew in Illinois? I never made any connection!" Don was as dumbfounded as I had been when Grace told me about the artist and handed me Don's picture.

"A friend of mine bought one of your paintings some time back in Staley. You painted that picture of my old farm, didn't you?"

"Yes, I did. And I've been back there several times to paint scenes from Uncle Jack's farm and yours. It has brought back so many memories, Sophie, and I can't believe it's you on the phone!"

We talked for an hour about our lives since those days so long ago when Don was healing from a broken leg. We were like two teenagers, suspended in conversation and totally rapt in each other's stories.

"Sophie, where do you live? Are you here in Iowa?" Don seemed anxious to see me and talk to me on a different plain.

"I live in Chatsworth. Do you know where that is?"

"I sure do. When might be a good time for us to get together? I'd really like to take you to dinner, but I'll need directions to your house. What do you say?"

We agreed on Friday evening at six-thirty, and I gave Don the directions from the highway to my house. I reluctantly ended the conversation, pointing out how pleased I was to have made contact with him.

I hung up the phone with my hand trembling and my heart racing. I was sure my face was flushed with excitement at seeing Don again. Friday was a whole five days away. I called Grace to tell her about the conversation.

"So you have a date?"

"Well, not exactly. It's just a dinner out to talk about old times and catch up on things."

"Sounds like a date to me!" Grace delighted in teasing me about the dinner plans, feeling my excitement about the meeting.

I was again feeling exhausted from all the excitement of the day. I mechanically moved through my nightly routine of cream applications, slipped into my nightgown, and crawled between the sheets. Before I turned out the light, I opened the drawer in the nightstand beside the bed. The ring and chain were still there in the box Don had given me so long ago. I would have to remember to put them in my purse before Friday night.

Chapter 20
THE STORY CONTINUES

I am told that Don couldn't wait to share his very interesting weekend with his artist friends. "I'm telling you, it was the most incredible phone call I have ever received. I had just talked with this woman a few hours before at the airport in Chicago, and I didn't even introduce myself. We were just making stranger small talk, you know?"

"Let me get this straight. You knew who she was, but you didn't know who she really was?" asked one of the students.

That's right. I knew she was Sophie Lincoln, the author who is coming to Staley to the bookstore, but I didn't know that she was the same Sophie I had known when I was a kid at my uncle's farm in Illinois!" Don was animated in his description of their encounter. "Now that I know who she is, I can see the girl in her. We are going to get together on Friday for dinner."

Everyone was interested in their friend's enthusiasm for this new lady in his life. "Have you read any of her books?"

Don gave them a passing glance, and then grinned sheepishly. "I have, but they aren't my genre; they're women's fiction. But there's something delightful about the fact that she writes from the 'Midwest' approach. I don't think her newest one is any different, but I need to read at least a part of it before we get together, so I have a feel for the story, and for Sophie's writing."

"That sounds like a good idea, Buddy. Has she seen any of your paintings?"

"Evidently she has a friend who has purchased two of them. One is the landscape I sold at the contest way back in November, and the other is one of my cat, sold last weekend at the art exhibit. She said she almost fainted when she saw the landscape, because it's of the farm in Illinois where she grew up. The whole thing is unbelievable."

Don's mind was far away to a time many years before in the summer of his youth. It was hard to focus on his work.

Thursday was an unseasonably warm day. Don's son, Marty, called his dad to see if he might be up for a golf match, and was pleased to get a positive response. The two of them met at the country club and enjoyed playing just the nine-hole range. Don found himself surprisingly winded on the way up the hill toward the club house. Feeling a little sick to his stomach, he sat down on a bench in the locker area and leaned back against the wall. He was also feeling some chest pains.

"Dad, are you feeling okay?" asked Marty, placing a hand on his shoulder.

"I'll be fine. I just need to catch my breath. It must be something I ate, because I'm having some indigestion, too." He took a couple of deep breaths, trying to alleviate the tightness in his chest.

Marty dropped him off at the house, but was relieved to hear that Don had an appointment the next day at the doctor's office.

On Friday morning, Don went to his appointment at 10:00. He had been feeling some pain in his left arm in addition to the incident from yesterday, so was anxious to discuss it with the doctor. He had always considered himself to be in good health, always passing his exams and blood tests with no real issues. His blood pressure was a little high when he had taken it at the pharmacy on occasion, but he figured those weren't always as accurate as they should be.

The doctor's office had a faint odor of alcohol as he entered the waiting room. He signed in on the clipboard and took a chart from the receptionist to complete with any updated information. The waiting room was cheerfully decorated, with framed posters of scenes from Paris in the spring. Magazines were in disarray on the tables, since a number of patients had already preceded him earlier in the morning. He checked his insurance card number against the preprinted information on his chart, noted the spelling and the street address, and handed the chart back through the open window.

Within a few minutes, a nurse opened the door and called him into the office, where he was first directed to a scale to be weighed. The nurse then handed him a small paper cup and instructions for providing a urine specimen for testing. That completed, he was again shown to a smaller waiting area, where two other patients were already seated. "This is so time consuming," Don mentioned to another patient. There was a chuckle and a nod in response.

When it was finally his turn to be taken to an examining room, he winced from the pain in his left arm as he stood to follow the nurse, again feeling that wave of nausea. In the examining room, the nurse noted his blood pressure and directed him to strip down to his shorts for the doctor.

Doctor Flanigan opened the door to greet Don, reaching out with his right hand in welcome. "Good to see you, Don," he said.

"Doc." Don enjoyed the Irish brogue and sparkling eyes of the physician. Doc Flanigan had taken care of Arlene, along with her oncologist, and had been a big comfort to Don as he cared for her.

Doctor Flanigan took out his stethoscope and placed it on Don's chest and back, instructing him to take deep breaths. It seemed to Don that this procedure took longer than usual.

"Tell me, Don, have you had any problems with breathing, or with pain?"

"I'm having some pain right now in my left arm. And yesterday, I had an upset stomach and some chest pains."

"Lie back on the table for me, if you would. I want to listen a little more closely."

Don lay back on the table and stretched out his legs. Doc was making him a little nervous. He watched his face as he continued to listen to his abdomen, his lungs, and his heart. A frown creased his brown and forehead.

"Don, your blood pressure reading is pretty high, and I am hearing some sounds in your circulatory system I don't like. We are going to set you up for an EKG here in the office, and see what that tells us."

Don was feeling a little uneasy about the doctor's reaction and the tests he was ordering. The nurse placed the patches and leads on his chest and watched as the machine printed out the heart rhythm. He waited once again for Doc Flanigan to return to the room.

"Don, I want you to go over to the hospital to meet with the cardiologist there. I've already called ahead for him to meet you. His name is Doctor Ames. I'm going to call an ambulance to take you to the emergency area. You are showing signs of heart blockage, and I don't want to take any chances."

Don was alarmed by the concern in Doc Flanigan's voice. "I'll do whatever you say, Doc." He could see that this wasn't a time to argue about driving there by himself.

"I see that Marty's number is in your medical records here. I'll have the nurses give him a call to tell him what's going on, if that's okay with you." Again that no-nonsense attitude.

Don dressed and lay back down on the examining table as directed. The ambulance arrived and the EMTs loaded Don onto a gurney and pushed him out to the waiting vehicle. The hospital was a short distance away, but the EMTs provided oxygen for Don to ensure his breathing.

At the hospital, two attendants took him directly to the heart cath lab, had him undress and put on a gown, and set up the equipment. Dr. Ames talked to him briefly, explaining how the catheters are inserted into the leg artery, dye is injected into the arteries, and they are able to see if there is blockage in the heart. Don felt the whole situation surreal. He had been feeling fine, had continued his walking, and had even trekked back into the timber at the farm. Now these people were all handling him with kid gloves, as though he were on the brink of disaster.

Outside the lab, still lying on the gurney, Marty caught up with him.

"What's up, Dad?" he asked.

"I guess we will know soon enough. I just went in for my physical, and all of a sudden I'm being wheeled into an ambulance and into this testing lab. Doc says he thinks I have some blockage in my heart, and they can't take any chances. It's pretty scary!" He reached for Marty's hand and grasped it.

"Let me see what I can find out. If they move you, I'll catch up, okay?" Marty went down the hall to the nurses' station and leaned onto the counter to talk to a nurse.

While Marty was gone, a nurse came toward Don.

"Mr. Ribold, we are going to take you to a patient waiting room, until we get the results back from the tests. Someone will be there to talk to you soon." The nurse wheeled him to a waiting room area, where large recliners were set up behind drawn curtains, with a television mounted in each cubicle. She helped Don down from the gurney and into the recliner, and covered him with a warm blanket. The room felt cold to Don, so the blanket was a welcome relief.

It was already one o'clock in the afternoon. He had been with medical people for three hours already. And where was Marty?

"Hey, Dad. Are you feeling okay?" Marty pulled back the curtain and sat in a chair beside the recliner.

"I really don't feel all that bad, Marty. What did you find out?"

"The nurses told me that the cardiologist would take the information from the test, will talk with Doc Flanigan, and then they will talk to us. We should hear something soon."

The two of them sat silently for a few minutes, not knowing what to think of this unusual situation. Marty had always seen his dad as invincible, so the idea that he might be in danger was a new revelation. And Don was still in shock at the idea that he might have heart blockage. Could he die from it? Maybe a heart attack?

The curtains parted to reveal Doctor Flanigan and another man, dressed in hospital green. "This is Doctor James Cohen. He's a cardiovascular surgeon here at St. Andrews, and he can tell you about the findings from the tests." Doctor Flanigan did the introductions.

"Good afternoon, Mr. Ribold. I have to tell you that we are certainly thankful that you came into Doctor Flanigan's office for your physical this morning, or you could be in a very serious state. You have some major blockage in three of your main arteries. It is our opinion that we need to perform surgery on these as soon as possible, this afternoon. You have had a mild heart attack, and delaying the surgery could put you at serious risk for one more severe. With your permission, we will schedule this right away and prepare you for surgery." Doctor Cohen waited for Don's response.

Don looked from one doctor to the other, looking for some sign of hope. "And what do you see as the outcome of this surgery?" he asked.

"Complete recovery," Doctor Cohen responded. "You have some healthy tissue and you are basically in good physical condition, so I foresee no problems with your recovery. You will be somewhat limited for a time as the incisions heal, but I suspect that you will be feeling better in a month or so than you have felt for years. The blockages tend to wear away at your physical strength and ability, and you just get used to having limitations. Do you have a power of attorney for health care and a living will completed?"

This time Marty answered the question. "Yes, sir, we do have one. I am Don's son, Marty, and I have those documents. Do you need them right away?"

"Once we take Don into surgery, Marty, you can get them and bring them back with you to the hospital. He will be in surgery for several hours, then in the recovery room. The nurses will direct you to the waiting area, and we will keep you informed of our progress, as well as when we move him from one area to another." Dr. Cohen was very empathetic and comforting.

Don looked at Dr. Flanigan. "Doc, whatever you say, that's what we'll do.

"Don, you really need to have this surgery performed right away. The risk will be minimized now while we have you right here."

"Okay, then. Let's do it." Don leaned his head back against the head rest of the recliner and gripped the arm rests. Marty reached out and covered his dad's hand with his own.

For the next hour, nurses came and went from Don's cubicle area, starting IVs, setting up monitoring equipment and shaving his chest. The anesthesiologist came to talk to him about what to expect from the anesthetics administered during surgery.

At about three-thirty the attendants came to help Don onto a cart, covered him with a warm blanket and wheeled him out of the waiting area. He watched overhead as they moved under the lights and into an elevator. Then they moved through sets of doors and into a room where the air felt cold and lights overhead were very bright. The doctor was there with his head covered, glasses on his nose, and a mask on his face. Don only recognized him from the eyes. The anesthesiologist told Don he would be going to sleep, and he would be awakened in the recovery room. Just before he fell asleep, he thought about the day and the date and his plans for the evening. *Sophie!*

"Don! Can you hear us now?" Everything was a haze. He felt himself trembling, feeling cold and clammy. He couldn't wake up, and drifted off.

"Don, we are in the recovery room, and your surgery is over. Open your eyes, Don. It's time to wake up." More talking. Don's mouth felt dry, his lips and tongue like there were covered with glue. He turned his head from side to side, trying to shake off the sleep. He drifted off again.

"Okay, Don. We are out of surgery now, and you are waking up from the anesthetic. Can you talk to us?"

"Yes," Don spoke barely above a whisper. This heaviness was hard to come through. "I'm waking up."

"Don, if you can stay awake for a little while, we can get you to your room, and you can go back to sleep there. Are you with us?"

He felt himself coming around to be more aware of his surroundings. Nurses in green shirts, green caps, and white masks moved around him. The room was brightly lit and sterile in appearance. He struggled to keep his eyes open, even if just enough to peek through to see what was going on around him. Was it over already? Hadn't he just gone to sleep?

"There you go. Now you are coming back to us." The nurse leaned over him to see that his eyes were opening. "Everything is looking good, Don. We are going to take you back to your room now, okay?"

"Yes." Again Don was able to just make out a whisper in response to the nurse's questions. "Looking good? What? Oh, yes, the surgery," he remembered. He tried to move his arm to his chest, but his arm felt very heavy. He felt the cart begin to roll and was once again watching the lights above him, the doors as they passed through, the elevator, and finally a hallway and into a room.

"You are on the cardiac wing, Mr. Ribold. You'll be in the intensive care area for at least one day, and we will then move you to a room of your own as you do your rehab. You'll be back fit as a fiddle in no time!" The nurse was cheerful and encouraging.

Don wasn't interested. "Just let me sleep," he thought.

An attendant came into the room to assist the nurse in moving Don from the cart to the bed. For the first time, Don felt pain from his surgery and whimpered as they slid his body onto the bed. The nurse covered him with a sheet, then brought another warm blanket, checked his IV fluid bags, and took his pulse before leaving him in the room. Once again, sleep overtook him, and he was lost to the reality of his situation.

"Dad? Dad, can you hear me?" Marty was stunned to see all the tubes and wires attached to his father, seeing him more vulnerable than he could ever remember.

"Hi, Marty," Don managed, again feeling the effects of the anesthesia and struggling to wake up.

"They tell me things went really well in surgery. The areas where there was blockage have been repaired.

The outlook is good, and they think you will make a complete recovery."

"I don't feel so chipper at the moment," Don said, smiling a thin smile to reassure Marty that he was going to be okay. Then he drifted off again into the sleep that seemed to take his mind into oblivion, never to return.

Marty watched Don sleeping, looking from one monitor to another, wondering what all of them meant. A nurse came into the room to look at them as well. Seeing that Marty was just waiting for his father to open his eyes again, she briefly explained to Marty the meaning of the various readings and what they would be expecting as he recovered from the surgery.

Don opened his eyes again, and saw that Marty was still there. It seemed that each time he woke up, he was a little more aware of his surroundings. But then the sleep would overtake him again.

"Thanks for being here, Marty,"

"I'll be hanging around for a while, until I'm sure you are doing okay." But Marty could see that he had again drifted off. He stepped out of the room and walked down the hall and down the elevator to the second floor. There a cafeteria served a buffet of food and drinks. He chose an apple and a donut, along with a cup of coffee, and sat at a table. The whole experience had left him feeling strange emotions about his father. Thank God, he was going to be okay, and Marty would still have time with him. What if he had had a fatal heart attack? What if he had a stroke and was permanently disabled? For the first time, Marty felt an overwhelming responsibility and a dependency on his dad that he had not acknowledged for some time. He finished his snack and returned to Don's room, taking Don's hand in his as he stood beside his bed watching him.

Don opened his eyes again and looked at his son.

"What time is it, Marty?"

Marty looked at his watch. "It's about 7:30. It's been a long day.

"I need for you to do something for me. On the counter in my condo is a card with a phone number on it for Sophie Lincoln. Would you please call her and tell her what's happened? I was supposed to see her this evening at 6:30. Don't ask questions; it's a long story. And I need for you to get my neighbor to take care of Hope. I don't know how long I'll be in here."

Marty smiled at Don's sleepy instructions. And who was this Sophie?

"I'll go by the condo when I leave here, and take care of things there for you. Anything else you need?"

"Maybe I'll think of something tomorrow, but right now I can't stay awake. You just go on ahead, and you can check on me later, okay? And thanks again for being here, Marty." Don squeezed his hand.

Marty leaned over to embrace his dad. "I'll be back in the morning." He stopped by the nurses' station to let them know he was leaving and went on to take care of the orders Don had given him. He would have to make some arrangement for the cat with his dad's neighbor, and then he would make the call to Sophie Lincoln. What was that all about?

The drive to Don's condo gave Marty some to think about how grateful he was that Don had come through the surgery. In the past several years they had become very close, united in life by the death of his mother and his sister.

Chapter 21

SOPHIE'S STORY CONTINUES

I was delighted to be able to get back into the yard to work on the perennials, clean out all the late fall leaves, and prepare the garden area for plantings. I could get in some radishes and carrots, as well as some potatoes at this early stage of spring. The marigolds had to be cut back, and the dead leaves removed from the hosta shoots and other spring flowering plants. I dragged out some planters from the shed to wash down and fill with potting soil. The top of the bird bath was heavy, but I managed to roll it out to the stand, then boost it onto the pedestal. The birds would enjoy the fresh water in the early spring sunshine.

The garden center was already lined with hundreds of plants for early spring planters. Since the price was right, I loaded up a number of plants into the trunk of the car, planning to place them in the shed for a couple more weeks to make sure there were no more frosts. I picked up some vegetable seeds and flower seeds, along with some gladiola bulbs, and found a new garden rake to replace the old one with the broken handle.

Tuesday night, I ran a hot tub of water to soak away the aches in my muscles from the bending and squatting. On Wednesday night, I looked into the closet to see what was appropriate to wear to my dinner with Don. Everything looked old to me, and I wanted to have something that was bright and springy.

"Grace, want to go shopping with me?" I asked, calling early the next morning.

"Sure, I'm always up for that, you know. You want to go today?"

"Yes. I need a new dress for tomorrow night, and my closet is looking very sad and stoic. I'm sure you can help me find something more appropriate."

The two of us had a good time shopping, stopped for lunch, and managed to find two new outfits to compliment this mop of graying red hair, as well as a new pair of shoes for spring. Grace was enjoying my enthusiasm about the 'date' with Don.

On Friday, I again worked in the yard, but left in the late morning to have my nails done, along with a pedicure. I worked on some promotional materials in the afternoon, organizing my presentations for the book signings that were coming up, as the day seemed to drag on. My mind was constantly distracted, thinking about seeing Don again and talking about old times. I was anxious to hear about his family and curious about the apparent tragedies they had endured. How sad to have lost a child, then to lose a spouse as well.

I showered and dressed, put on one of the new outfits, and fussed with my hair. As six-thirty approached, I began to watch for Don's car to pull up outside the house.

Six thirty-five, six forty, six forty-five.

I wondered if I had made a mistake in giving Don the directions to the house. Surely, he would not have decided not to come without calling. Could he have had an accident?

By seven, I felt very anxious and disappointed that the evening had come to this. I pushed back thoughts of being stood up, thinking instead that Don must have gotten detained somehow. I took out a small container of soup and heated it up in the microwave. Not exactly what I had planned to have for dinner. I hung up my clothes and slipped into my robe, curling up in the recliner.

Finally at eight o'clock the phone rang.

"Hello?" I was hoping to hear Don's voice on the other end of the line.

"My name is Marty Ribold. May I speak to Sophie Lincoln?"

"This is Sophie, Marty. Is everything okay?"

"Sophie, my dad asked that I call you. He's had a pretty rough day. We found out this morning that he had some serious blockage in arteries from his heart, and the doctors performed surgery this afternoon to open them up. The surgery is over, and he's doing fine, just lost for the moment in a haze of anesthetics."

"Oh, my!" I gasped. "That's terrible! Did he know he had some problems?"

"Evidently not. We played golf yesterday, and he was feeling a little short of breath and nauseous, but he chalked it up to something he had eaten. But when he went to the doctor this morning for a regular checkup, they got him to the hospital right away."

"I wonder if I might go to see him."

Marty hesitated. "He's in intensive care for now, but I suspect they will move him in the next day or so. Would you like for me to call you when they get him into a private room?"

"That would be great, Marty. Thank you."

"I haven't heard my dad mention you before, Sophie. Have you known each other long?"

"Longer than you can imagine, Marty. We just hadn't seen each other for a long time, and it's a long story. Maybe I'll run into you at the hospital, and I'll tell you all about it." I smiled, feeling anxious for Don, but somewhat relieved at knowing what had detained him.

Marty signed off with a promise to call me when Don was moved out of intensive care. After hanging up the phone, I immediately picked it up to call Grace.

"Grace, I've been stood up," I said, knowing how Grace would react.

"Well, so much for the nice gentleman from your childhood!" She was incensed to think that I had been left waiting. "Have you heard from this jerk at all?"

Grace's reaction made me laugh. "Easy there, Grace. Yes, I have heard from him through his son. The poor man went for a physical this morning and ended up in open heart surgery. He's in the hospital in Staley in intensive care. He had his son, Marty, call me to let me know what had happened."

"Oh, well, that's better. You could have told me that from the beginning. Is he going to be all right?"

I sat down on a kitchen chair and propped my feet up on a second one. "Marty says he came through the surgery in good shape. He had three blockages, which have all been repaired. Marty is going to call me when Don gets moved out of intensive care."

"So are you going to go see him?"

"Sure I will. He'll be laid up in the hospital for a while, and he'll be anxious for company, I'm sure."

We chatted for a few minutes more about the events of the week, until I finally ended the conversation. "I'll let you know when I hear from them."

It was Monday before I got a call again from Marty to let me know that his dad had been moved out of intensive care. He gave me the room number and assured me that Don would be anxious for company. There were already plans for Tuesday, but I decided that I would make the trip to Staley on Wednesday to see Don.

The hospital had recently undergone some renovation, and the entrance was open and cheerful. A volunteer at the reception desk directed me to the elevator to take me to the cardiac unit and Don's room. When I reached the doorway, I knocked lightly on the door, which was open about three inches.

"Don, are you in there?" I asked. "It's Sophie." I was speaking softly so as not to wake him if he were asleep.

"Yes, please come in," was the response from inside the room.

I pushed the door open slightly to see that Don was sitting up in his bed, watching the television on the opposite wall. I walked over toward him.

"Sophie! I'm so glad to see you, and I apologize for Friday night. In all the commotion here at the hospital, I forgot all about our plans for the evening, and thought of you just as they were putting me under the anesthetic."

"Well, I'm just glad you are doing well. Marty tells me you are making a remarkable recovery from the surgery."

"Please come sit here by me, and let's catch up on what has been going on in our lives since we saw each other last. How many years has it been?"

I pulled a chair closer to the bed and took off my jacket, pulling it over the back of the chair.

"Can I get you anything?" I asked Don.

He smiled. "No thanks. They wait on me hand and foot in here, so I'm already getting spoiled."

I grinned at him mischievously. "You know, this is getting a little old. The last time I saw you, you were also immobile!"

For the next hour the two of us shared memories of time together in Illinois, of Don's marriage and children, and of my family. I asked him about his daughter, and found that Annie's death had been a hard time for him and his wife, Arlene. Arlene and my husband Carl had both experienced long illnesses before their deaths. We talked about happy times and shared stories of children and grandchildren. Don told me about his art work, and I rambled on about writing. We found many mutual interests in music and the arts.

"Don, I really have to get going, as I have a meeting back in Chatsworth later this afternoon. Can I come back to visit you again?"

He reached for my hand as I stood up beside the bed.

"I'll be heartbroken if you don't come back. I'm sure I'll be here for a while yet. They have me in therapy already, though."

I wasn't anxious to pull away from him, but reluctantly reached for my jacket and purse.

I'll call you before I come back, maybe this weekend?"

"That would be wonderful, Sophie. Remember you used to read to me? I'd like that." He smiled, his eyes sparkling.

"I'll see you then." I walked out the door and turned to look back at him once more, waving good-bye as I started down the hall. The moment felt like walking on air, and I almost felt guilty as I passed a mirror on the wall and saw my reflection. I turned quickly away, smiling broadly, and quickening my steps down the hall to the elevator. Outside the first floor, it seemed as though the birds were singing louder than before, and the air was filled with the aroma of spring blossoms, just breaking out on the trees around the hospital.

I returned to visit Don on Sunday afternoon, then again on the following Wednesday. Don was released from the hospital that next Friday and gave me directions to his home, along with an invitation to come to visit him there. On Saturday, I arrived at his condo with bags of groceries, ready to prepare some food for the day, as well as to put together some things that would be easy for him to heat up. He helped me chop vegetables and wash dishes, resting occasionally at my insistence.

Hope the cat was immediately accepting. She rubbed against my legs as I prepared food, purring loudly. Finally, I removed my apron, and sat down in a chair across from the recliner where Don rested.

"The apple pie is in the oven, so we can have dinner in about an hour," I said, enjoying the chance to sit down for a few minutes.

Don studied me for a moment. "You have been working in here for a couple of hours! Supper smells delicious. And that pie will be out of this world, I just know it."

I could feel myself blushing at his comment. "It feels good to sit down."

Don got up from the recliner and walked to the sofa. "Come sit here beside me." He patted the cushion on the couch. I got up from the chair and joined him. He put his arm around me, and I leaned back against it.

"I can't tell you how much I've enjoyed your company this last couple of weeks, Sophie. As soon as I'm able to drive, we'll go out for that dinner we missed out on."

I turned toward him. "I've enjoyed the time as well, Don. And I'm so glad you are feeling better. That was not an easy surgery to go through."

Don laid his hand over mine, drawing it to him, and kissing my fingers. We sat for a few moments in silence, Hope finally jumping up between us and settling down on Don's leg. Her purring was the only sound in the room.

"Sophie, it's been a long time since I felt I wanted to kiss a woman. May I kiss you?"

I felt like a teenager with butterflies in my stomach. The whole scene felt strangely surreal. I turned toward him, and leaned in to receive the kiss. His lips were warm and moist, and he pressed them gently but firmly against mine. We parted, and I melted against the back of the sofa. My heart was pounding in my chest, and I was sure that Don could hear it.

"Can you hear my heart pounding?" I asked, smiling at him.

"No, because mine is making more noise, and I'm afraid it actually could burst the incision!" He grinned at me with that mischievous smile, his eyes dancing.

"Don, I'm not sure if I'm ready for this."

"Let's just take it one day at a time. We enjoy each other's company, and we have so much in common. What do you say?"

"I think that's a great idea. And for right now, we have supper ready, so let's eat!"

We enjoyed the dinner, and the apple pie for dessert, sipping a glass of wine, and then enjoying coffee. I put leftovers in special containers for Don to warm up while he was at the condo by himself. Then I wrapped the leftover pie with cellophane, put the dishes in the dishwasher, and tidied up the kitchen, while Don perched on a stool visiting with me.

When it was time for me to leave, he walked me to the door, and kissed me tenderly once again.

"It will be lonely here without you tomorrow, Sophie," he said as he released me. "When will you be back?"

"I'll call you when I get back home and can look at my calendar, but I think I can make it back on Tuesday. That's just a couple of days away." I was as anxious to return as Don was to have me.

As I drove back to Chatsworth on the darkened highway, I thought about Don's words, "Let's just take one day at a time." I felt comforted by those words, unsure of what my feelings were for Don at this moment.

In the darkness, I drove out to the cemetery, which was well-lit by the street lamps surrounding it. At Carl's grave, I stopped the car and got out, walking toward the headstone. Tears streamed down my face as I felt an overwhelming sense that I had betrayed Carl. Except for some very brief romances before we had met, Carl had been the only man with whom I had shared true love. He was the father of my children, and the man who had cared for me all those years. And now, in the short span of two weeks, I had feelings for a man I barely knew, and who apparently was feeling the same way about me. How could this be?

Just as suddenly as I had been overcome with grief, I felt a sense of relief. It was as though Carl was telling me to move on with my life. I walked back to the car and drove home in silence, hearing Don's words, "Let's just take one day at a time."

Chapter 22
SOPHIE'S FINAL CHAPTER

Spring quickly turned to summer, as Don completed his therapy following his surgery. I had the flower garden in full bloom, the roses climbing the fence in the back, and the perennials all bearing their fragrant flowers. The flower urns were planted with vines and a variety of brilliant summer colors in full bloom. The days were much warmer, and the evenings cooled just enough to require a sweater outside.

Don had made several trips to see me, enjoying my home and cooking, and enjoying everything about the woman he had known as a girl so long ago. Shirley had stopped by for lunch one day when Don was there, and after meeting him, had given me approval of this new friend. Shirley had no idea of how serious our relationship had become.

"Sophie, I still owe you a nice dinner out, remember? You have been doing all the work, cooking for me and making sure I have plenty of food stocked up at home. Where would you like to go?"

I looked at Don and smiled. It was so nice that he was appreciative of the help I had given him. "I think I'd like seafood. Do you know of a place?"

"As a matter of fact, I do. But it's out a ways, by a lake near Green Meadow, where Arlene and I lived when the kids were younger. If you are interested, I'll make a reservation."

I walked to my calendar to check on the schedule. I would be traveling this coming weekend, but would be in town the following week. "How about a week from Saturday? Does that fit into your plans?"

Don pulled out his pocket organizer to check the dates, and we agree on the date. "I need to get back home today, as I have a class to go to tonight." He rose from the chair by the table and crossed the kitchen to put his arms around me. He kissed me lightly, and then kissed me again, pressing his lips firmly against mine. He held me close, and I offered no resistance.

"Sophie, you are an amazing woman, and I'm falling in love with," Don said, as he drew back from me, looking deeply into my eyes. "Don't say anything just yet. I really have to go now, but I'll call you later on this week, before you leave for San Francisco." He gave me one more hug, then was out the door before I even had a chance to reply.

I watched him get into his car and drive away, waving as his car pulled into the street. He awoke feelings in me that I hadn't felt in so long, and it was good to know that he was interested in me as a woman, as well as being a friend. I fanned myself with the kitchen towel, as I thought about his kiss and the moment he had held me so closely. Was it possible that I might be ready to share another man's bed? The thought seemed almost natural to me, as I was quite sure of the feelings for Don.

We had made a pitcher of iced tea, and I poured myself a glass. I had been thinking of writing another book, and was starting to put together the outline of it, not quite sure how I was going to approach the characters and the story line. With these new feelings for Don raging inside me, it was hard to concentrate on the task at hand. I wondered what his body was like. The hair on his chest was thick and gray, and his arms were strong. He had a good shape for a man his age, muscular and tall, and he was so gentle with me. I thought about how his jeans fit him, and I felt myself warming with the thought of him physically.

"I'm too old to be thinking about sex," I said to myself, smiling at my arousal. I was quite sure that if he caught me at a weak moment, and had intentions of being in my bed, I would not resist. I stood up and looked at myself in the mirror, turning for a side view, and sucking in my stomach.

I kept busy the rest of the week and caught the plane to San Francisco for the book signings there. My friend, Joy, picked me up at the airport and shuttled me around on Friday and Saturday, while I made my appearances. Don had called on Wednesday night before I left, not mentioning what he had declared to me at the house. I shared my feelings with my friend, Joy.

"Joy, he has made me feel alive again, and I'm even considering what it would be like to sleep with him!"

Joy laughed at me. "Sophie, I have to tell you that when I got my divorce, I thought I'd never be interested in a man physically again. But that all changes. We aren't meant to be alone, and having a good man to share a physical relationship can be great. Don sounds like just such a guy."

At that moment it occurred to me that I might consider interviewing other women my age who had experiences in losing a mate to either death or divorce, and how they managed to go on with their lives. It would be interesting for me, and other readers might find some hope for the future when they are in such a situation.

"Joy, would you be willing to talk candidly while I take notes on how you got back into the mainstream after your divorce? I'm thinking it might be interesting reading. I'd use a fictitious name, of course."

"Sure, I have no problem with that. I think that if I had read something about other women's experiences, it would have been helpful to me. How many would you think you would have to interview?"

Joy and I discussed the possibilities of the book, and how it would be received. We both thought of it as an interesting topic with some reader appeal. I decided to pitch the idea to Angie to see what her reaction might be. The San Francisco Bay area was so beautiful in June. The bougainvillea vines were in full bloom, their brilliant flowers cascading down walls and rooftops. The ice flowers populated the hillside. The morning fog was lifting, giving me a view of the Golden Gate Bridge and Alcatraz Island as the plane nosed up into the clouds. On Sunday, I returned to Iowa, bidding Joy goodbye with a promise to return soon. My thoughts were once again back to Don.

Don told me he attended his class, as he did every week, but this time shared the new love in his life with his friends. He felt euphoric thinking of me, as I had become such an important part of his life. The doctors had told him he would find renewed energy and stamina following his rehabilitation after the surgery. But Don really felt that his relationship with me had contributed to his new attitude on life. His art work was selling in a few local shops, including the bookstore in his neighborhood.

Don also said he wanted more from our relationship. He wanted to be with me every day of the week. He wanted to hold me and feel my body next to his in his bed. After Arlene's death, the idea of being with another woman had been far from his wildest imagination. If he asked me, would I marry him? He was still young at heart, and now he had a new lease on life. While walking his route on Thursday morning, he decided to stop in the jewelry store to look at rings, just in case he decided to purchase one.

"May I help you?" The clerk had Don in his sights as soon as he came through the door.

"I'm not sure. I have a lovely lady in my life, and I'd like to look at rings. I've pretty much decided to take a chance and ask her to marry me, but I don't know for sure that she will agree." Don smiled at the clerk, who was obviously amused at his apprehension.

The clerk walked around to the inside of the display cases, and pulled out a tray of rings from the end of the counter to show them to Don. "Do you have any idea about size or color?" he asked, gesturing toward the array of settings.

"I haven't even gotten that far. I'd say yellow gold, and probably a pretty conservative setting, knowing Sophie."

"And would you like a round diamond, or a pear shaped one?"

The questioning continued for some time, as the clerk tried to surmise the ring that would be the most appropriate for the customer's lady friend.

"Here's what we can do to make this easier for you. You pick out a ring that you like, and we'll start from there. If she agrees to marry you, then she can bring in the ring, and we can reset the stone in whatever mounting she likes, based on a price range we agree to. How does that sound?"

"That would be great! This is just too much pressure!" Don was relieved at the clerk's solution. They looked through a number of settings and settled on one Don thought I might like. It was gold with a round diamond with two small diamonds on either side of the main stone. The wedding band was plain, and there was a matching one for him. Could he even speculate that he would be back into the store to select the wedding bands as well?

"I'll get this ready for you, and you can pick it up tomorrow morning, if that will be soon enough for you."

"Oh, yes. We have plans for tomorrow night, so the timing will be perfect. I'll be back in the morning, and I'll bring my credit card along."

Don says he left the store feeling very nervous about his purchase. Had he completely lost his mind? Here he was, a man in his sixties, looking at starting over in a marriage with a woman he had fallen head over heels in love with in a matter of weeks. He walked the remainder of his route back to his condo. There he shared with Hope his plans for Friday night.

"If she agrees, little buddy, we will be sharing our life with Sophie!" He cuddled the kitten, stroking her as she purred loudly.

Don arrived at my house a little early, and we shared a glass of wine before leaving for dinner. We talked about the trip to San Francisco, and about Don's progress in his rehab on the way to the restaurant.

"I'm so excited for you that you are really beginning to feel stronger, Don. I'm sure you are glad it's behind you."

"I can really tell the difference in my stamina. I'm walking farther each day, and really enjoying the summer weather. I don't think I could have done it without you, Sophie."

I blushed and smiled at him. This man could melt my heart with one glance or one compliment.

We arrived at the restaurant right on time and were seated with a view of the lake almost immediately. There was an air of elegance about the place, mixed with a more casual ambiance. We ordered drinks and studied the menu for just the right selection. The food was just as good as Don had remembered from many years ago and had related to me. How strange that he now would bring me here, where he and Arlene had eaten so many times before.

The waitress brought coffee and a dessert menu after we had finished eating. Once she was out of sight, Don reached across the table for my hand.

"Don, this was just delightful," I said, caressing his fingers with my thumb and looking into his eyes.

"Yes, it was. Sophie, I have something I'd like to talk to you about."

"Okay." I felt a little concerned, not sure what to expect.

"We've had some good times together since you came to see me at the hospital. I really hope we can continue to enjoy each other's company."

"Oh, I've enjoyed this time as much as you," I commented.

"Please let me finish, and then I'll be looking for your thoughts." He squeezed my hand, and I waited for him to continue.

"I never dreamed I would be interested in spending time with another woman in my life. But here you are, and my life has taken on a whole new meaning. Yesterday I went into a jewelry store on my walk, and I bought something for you." He reached into his pocket and pulled out the ring box, opening it for me to see the contents.

"Sophie, will you marry me?"

I was complete caught off guard. I knew that my feelings for Don were getting stronger every day, but I had not expected a proposal. I looked at the ring, and then looked at Don, then back to the ring.

"It's so beautiful!" I exclaimed, looking in to Don's eyes, so full of love and sweetness. "Yes, I will!"

"You will? I can't believe it! I had all sorts of speeches ready to make to convince you that we could get married." He stood up and pulled me to my feet, kissing me firmly on the lips. Then he turned to the restaurant crowd and said, "She said 'yes'!"

Everyone broke into applause for the happy couple. I was blushing again as we sat back down.

"Let's get married right away, what about it?" he asked.

"I can hardly catch my breath. There is so much to talk about, Don. Your son, my kids and grandkids, our friends, will all want to be a part of this, won't they?"

"I know there is a lot to think about. If you want to do something local, that's fine with me, but I'd like to take a trip, maybe a cruise, and get married there. Doesn't that sound like fun?"

I had never done anything so spontaneous in my life. But I was completely excited about the idea. It would be so different from all the traditional trappings, and it would probably be easier on the kids not to have to go through the wedding hoopla.

"It does sound like fun, so let's do it." I was almost giggling.

We finished our coffee and a light dessert, and headed back for my house, talking all the way about plans for the wedding. I put on a pot of coffee at the house, and we sat down on the couch to talk more about all the plans. Don got up, walked over to the CD player and put on some music.

"Let's dance, my love," he said, taking my hand. "We can make plans another time."

He held me close to him, putting both arms around me, and we swayed to the music. The kisses grew longer and more intense, our bodies responding to the embrace and the movement.

"Stay the night with me," I whispered, kissing him lightly on the neck and taking in the smell of his aftershave.

He held me to him and moved his hand up my side to brush against the side of my breast. "Are you sure?"

My breath caught at his touch, my body alive with feelings so long unfamiliar that I had nearly forgotten them. We turned off the music and the lights, and walked down the hall toward the bedroom hand in hand. The grandfather clock in the hallway chimed the hour, as Don closed the door behind us.

Chapter 23
THE STALEY BOOK SIGNING

When Sophie arrived at the bookstore in Staley for the book signing, Ben had a table set up for her, a stack of her books on the table, and an array of drinks and finger foods on a buffet on the wall between the bookshelves.

"You must be Sophie," he said, extending his hand to shake hers.

Sophie shifted her arm load of books to the other side, and returned the gesture. "I am, and you must be Ben. I'm really pleased to be here with you."

Ben showed her to the table where she would be sitting to greet customers. "I have advertised the readings and lecture to be at ten if that works out for you."

"That's fine, thanks. I see you already have some chairs set up. You have done a really nice job with this, Ben. Sometimes when I arrive at a bookstore, I still have to get everything in order. That's why I'm a little early." She looked at her watch and noted the time. "We still have a whole hour before you open."

Sophie wandered around the room, looking at the book shelves lined with books of various genres, and admiring the art work for sale on the walls.

"These are by Don Ribold," Sophie mentioned. She noted the illegible signature on the familiar acrylic.

"Yes, they are. Don comes in here quite often and lives just a short distance away. He bought one of your books last week, even though he said it wasn't his usual reading choice."

Sophie smiled and accepted a cup of coffee from Ben. "I knew Don when we were children in Illinois."

"That's what I understand, and your story begins around those times, right?"

"Yes, it does." Sophie walked away again, continuing to peruse the book titles. She heard the tinkling of the bell on the door, indicating that she and Ben were no longer alone. She looked down the aisle of the bookshelves to see if she could see who had entered, but caught only a glimpse of a man walking toward Ben at the front of the store.

Then she heard him speak. "Is she here yet?" Sophie suspected it was someone Ben knew and had allowed in to meet the author a little early.

"Yes, she is. Sophie? Can you come to the front of the store?"

Sophie made her way back through the book shelving to the table Ben had set up for her. She set her coffee down on the table and sat in the chair. Not until then did she look up to see the customer who had come in. He was tall and dark complexioned, with a wave in his graying hair. His eyes sparkled as he walked toward her, carrying her book in his hand.

"Sophie Lincoln, you are a fraud!" he said sternly, his brow furrowing as he spoke to her, gripping her book in his hand.

"I beg your pardon? I'm sorry, sir, but I never claimed it was a true story. It's a fictional romance, and parts of it are based on a true story. Tell me, did you like the book?" Sophie was trying to see if the customer was really angry, or was just trying to be a pain.

The customer took a step back, and his frown turned to a smile. "Yes, I liked the book. Sophie, I'm Don Ribold."

Sophie was glad she was sitting down, as he had caught her completely by surprise. She had known there was a possibility of him arriving at the book signing, but was not expecting to see him so early in the morning. She rose from her chair and stretched out a hand to greet him.

"Don, so good to see you after all these years. I feel like we have been just missing each other here in Staley. I have a friend who has a painting of yours, and she told me she had found out that you were living here in Staley. Will you have some time to do some catching up today sometime?"

Don returned her greeting. "Sure, I'll be in and out all day, but how about if we get together over lunch?"

"My friend's coming from Chatsworth to meet me for lunch, but you are welcome to join us. Grace would enjoy meeting you."

They agreed on the time, and chatted only briefly about the missed chances of their meeting before now. Customers were beginning to arrive at the store, and Sophie began chatting with them and signing purchased copies of her book. At ten she gave a small lecture on writing and finding an agent and publisher, as well as reading excerpts from the story.

Grace arrived around eleven-thirty, and Sophie told her they were having lunch with Don Ribold. "Well, this should be interesting," said Grace, enjoying the mystique surrounding their past. Sophie had never really talked much about Don with Grace, preferring that Grace just enjoy the book.

Don arrived to escort them to lunch, and they left the store in Ben's hands until one-thirty. They walked to a small sandwich shop just a block away from the store.

"I usually go to the diner across the street, but I thought you ladies might enjoy the atmosphere here better." Don gestured to the surroundings in the quaintly decorated shop. The walls were a persimmon color and were adorned with posters from Broadway shows.

"They hold Improv Theater here on Saturdays, and have found quite a following for the plays." He pulled out two wrought iron chairs from the round table, allowing the ladies to sit down. "You can see the menu from here. What can I get for you?

Sophie and Grace gave him their preferences, and he walked to the counter to place the order.

"He is incredibly handsome!" giggled Grace, while she patted Sophie on the arm.

"Oh, Grace, you are incorrigible!"

"Nothing wrong with looking, Sophie. So that's the man that was once the boy you knew back on the farm in Illinois." Grace rubbed her chin. "What do you know about him?"

Sophie just shook her head. "I don't know anything about him, except that his wife and daughter died, and he has a son here in Staley. I found that out from an old friend at the diner back in Illinois. Shhhh! Here he comes!" Sophie pretended to be sharing just girl talk with Grace.

Don placed the tray of food in the center of the table, and pulled up a chair. Sophie reached into her purse to bring out a small box. She placed it in front of Don.

"I believe these belong to you," she said, smiling at him.

He opened the box to see the ring and chain. "I can't believe you still have these. You mention them in your book, and I can't for the life of me remember giving them to you. But what I am really curious about is how you came up with that story about the rain and the flood!"

Sophie laughed. "Well, I had to make it exciting for the readers. Do you think they would have been interested in how you fell off the tractor at your uncle's farm and broke your leg?"

"Let me get this straight," Grace began. "You mean that whole story about the flood and Donnie's rescue was made up?"

"Grace, I'm a writer. The idea is to create interest for the readers."

"Well, I knew you had made up the rest of your story, but I thought maybe the first part was based on reality." Grace finished her sandwich and sipped the last of her iced tea.

"The journals were real. But I had to create some excitement between the written lines of the journal. My life on the farm at ten and eleven years old was certainly less than exciting."

"So tell me about the broken leg, Don." Grace grinned at him.

"Like Sophie says, I fell off the tractor at my Uncle Jack's and broke my leg. Sophie did come over to read to me, and she wrote this poem." He took out a yellowing folded piece of paper from his wallet."

"You still have that?!" Sophie was amazed.

"I found it among some old things of mine when I was looking for my art supplies. You know how some things just never get thrown away?"

Grace stood up from her place at the small table. "I'm going to go browse around in the bookstore, and I'll see you two back there in a bit."

"Nice to meet you, Grace," said Don, standing as she walked away.

Sophie studied Don as he sat back down. "So what did you think of the rest of the story?" she asked, shifting in her seat.

"I can't figure out how you could be so accurate about my life, when you didn't even know for sure where I was."

"I found out about your wife, your son and daughter, as well as the fact that you were painting, from Jeff at the cafe. I also remembered that your mother was an artist, and that you had an interest in that as well. Grace had the painting of the farm, and even though we couldn't read your signature, I was sure you were the one who had painted it. I've been to the farm and the hideout as well. Then I did some research on the Internet to find out for sure about your son, and who had won the art contest in Staley at the college."

"Amazing. You are a very industrious woman, Sophie, and it's great to see you again."

"Listen, I need to get back to the bookstore this afternoon." Sophie stood up to leave.

"Will you wait for me there after the book signing? I'd like to spend a little more time with you, since I know very little about your life, and you evidently know a good deal about mine." Don reached for her arm. "I'll walk you back to the bookstore."

"Okay, Don. That would be nice. I should be finished by four o'clock." She hooked her arm through his, and they walked easily, retracing their route to the cafe.

At dinner that evening, Don and Sophie talked easily about their lives and their memories of that short time in the summer of their childhood. Don walked with her to her car, unlocked the door with her key fob, and helped her inside. She rolled down the window, after he had closed the door firmly.

"Will I see you again?" she asked.

He bent down and kissed her lightly. "Wild horses wouldn't keep me away. I'll call you this week. And, Sophie, we'll just take one day at a time."

***

ACKNOWLEDGEMENTS

I am always grateful to my wonderful husband, Jerry, for his patience with me and support in working to get my writing published. He has spent many hours looking at me from the back, as I'm focused on the computer in front of me. Also a special thanks to my family and friends who have read through the story and helped with some ideas: Jerry; my daughter, Heidi; friends Sue, Sharon and Joanie; and friend Carol in Georgia. A special thank you to WOW (Women of Words), my writer's group in Fredericksburg, Texas. You have all contributed to making my story ready for publication. Janie Goltz, your editing was such a great benefit to those who will read these words. Shelley Glasow Schadowsky wrestled with just the right appearance on the cover, which is amazing. Also, thanks to the family of AuthorHouse for all their support and guidance.

***

ABOUT THE AUTHOR

Linda Kay Christensen, a former farm girl from the central Illinois town of Delavan, has enjoyed many years as a bank manager, a self-employed accountant and tax preparer (CPA), and an online instructor for Keller Graduate School (DeVry University). She earned her bachelor's in Business Management and her Masters in Human Resources from the University of Illinois, Springfield. Linda's history in writing has included everything from business communication, teaching, and journaling, to occasional poetry and writing a daily blog. Her inspiration for "*Sophie Writes a Love Story*" comes from a series of five prints by C. Clyde Squires given to her grandmother in 1916 as a wedding gift. The people that the artist has created in these prints will come alive in Linda's series of the "five stages of love." Life in the time of the prints has changed dramatically, allowing for a new look at the stories behind a modern view of the prints.

Linda helped her mother, Wilma Diekhoff, complete her memoirs in a book that includes 200 recipes from family and friends. Wilma held a book signing at Barnes and Noble at the age of 82. *"Flavors from the Past: Memoirs and Recipes of Wilma Weiland Diekhoff"* is only available in digital format with various e-book publishers. Linda's first romance fiction novel was published in August of 2014. *"Annie's Love"* addresses mother love in its various interpretations. It is available in digital and print.

Linda is married to Jerry, a former engineer and now a master gardener. They live in Fredericksburg, Texas and have traveled extensively, meeting many of the characters who contribute to Linda's writings. She is a member of the Writers' League of Texas in Austin.

Follow Linda Kay at

http://senioradventureswithlindakay.blogspot.com